The Friendship Ruse

Georgia Tell

ISBN 978-0-9995788-0-3

Cover design by Camille
Published by Blue Hair Books

Visit author's website: www.GeorgiaTell.com
Follow author on Twitter: @GeorgiaTell

Thank you to Camille, Dianna, Kim, Alana and Stephanie.

I don't have friends, and I only half-know why.

Russell Jonson, some kid in my fifth period class, stopped at the table where I'd chosen to eat my food. I pulled my jacket close around my body and took a huge bite of my burrito from the truck that parked out by the front of school every Friday.

Russell was a pretty nice guy. He was on the football team and stood like five feet taller than my 5 feet 2 inches. He was one of the few people who acknowledged my existence and the only one to say 'hi' in passing. He was smiling, which was kind of what he did all the time. Imagine that, someone is actually happy. "Hi," he said.

"Hi." See? I did it right. I didn't start with some big honking expletive at the beginning of this — or any — social interaction.

"How's it going?"

"Good." Wow, I'm totally captivating and a great person to be around. My single syllable answer fell like a phone into a puddle of watery mud on a rainy day. I knew I should say something more, but as each micro-second ticked by, the silence grew bigger. *Geek, dork, outcast, lame couch potato*, I told myself. What was I doing? I had no idea. Someone was being nice to be me, and my big mouth had nothing to say.

"Okay," he said. "I'll see you around then."

"Bye," I was short with him. Maybe because I was filtering myself out of his league? I don't know. I knew he was too cool, too good-looking, too nice to be my friend. I imagined he was just giving me a second of his attention as a pity-party favor. In my mind, there was no way he was genuine. I was setting myself up for permanent failure in the friend department. He left. I focused on my burrito.

Denise Walker, head cheerleader (and, it was generally agreed, head drama queen), was about ten feet away from my table. She was pretty. Dark hair and dark eyes. Skinny, but nothing close to my stick figure status. Good height — taller than me, but, well, every-one is taller than me. "Hey," she said, smiling up at Dean Sexton. How's that for a name, Sexton? I couldn't make that up if I tried. She was standing unnaturally close to him. It made me want to remind her that I was sitting right there, that they weren't alone.

Dean, senior and student body president, leaned against my table. He was good-looking too. God, pretty attracts pretty. Where is there room in that for geeks like me? Darker hair than Denise's, and darker eyes. Taller. Muscled type of skinny. And really good-looking arms. I know that's a weird thing to notice, but they're like model arms. "Hey," he said, flashing Denise a Colgate bright smile. "So I'm going to San Francisco tonight for a show. You want to come with?"

Denise's eyes brightened, but her voice came out calm and composed and low, like she was trying to be ultra-sexy. "Sure, what time are you going to pick me up?"

"Seven."

"I'll be ready."

Dean walked off, and Denise collapsed onto the bench across from me. She smiled up at the sky like she'd just won the lottery. She covered her mouth and laughed. "Oh my god, how'd this happen?"

I grinned and answered, because I knew she wasn't talking to me — so naturally it was the time for my big mouth to make his appearance. "You're pretty people," I said.

Her head whipped around, and she was glaring at me like I'd peeped at her while she was changing — which, no, I've never done, I'm quite harmless, actually. "What?"

"I said that you two are pretty people, that's why he asked you out."

She shook her head. "It's not so superficial. Losers like you just think that, but it's because you're an ugly person inside and out. You just blame your outer appearance and other people, but really it's what's inside that counts."

Wow, she was snappy. Did she just call me an ugly person? Both inside and out? Even though she'd never said a word to me otherwise? "Nice, Denise, nice." I leaned forward and raised my eyebrows. "Do you even know my name?"

She looked surprised for a moment, but a grin spread across her face. "It's Rawley."

"That's my last name, Denise." I thought about it for a moment. "Lily is in cheerleading with you, so of course you'd know my last name." Lily was my asshole of a younger sister. It wouldn't be so bad having a younger sister if she was really little. But Lily's just a year younger than me, and because I must have some stunted growth or something, I'm shorter and generally weaker than her. I can't do those older brother noogies and tease her for being such a girly empty-headed bimbo, because she could just pound my face into a bloody mess on the pavement. Naw, she would never do that; she'd just hold me down and pinch me until I get bruises — which basically means, she'll be pinching me forever since I rarely bruise. I sighed, more depressed by that thought than I usually would be. "What's my first name, Denise Walker?"

She squinted her eyes. "This is so gay. You're stupid." She stood up.

"It's Warren. My name is Warren." I stood up, gathered my trash and grabbed my bag. "Don't tell me that I have a bad personality if you don't even know my name." And I walked away like a super cool actor who just revealed the most important bit of information, except I stumbled and the bell rang.

Yep, the rest of my Friday passed as I reveled in my glory. It didn't matter that Derek Jiracle made some joke at my expense during fifth period. It didn't matter that Benny Higald completely ignored my frantically waving hand when she asked for questions at the end of her presentation.

When the final bell rang, I walked home. My sister wasn't with me because she always had some cheer practice or something after school.

Mom was scrubbing the entranceway hardwood floor when I opened the door. "Hello, honey."

"Hi, Mom. Do you need to be doing that? It's pointless. Me 'n Lily are just gonna track some shi – dirt in." I caught myself swearing because my mom hates it with a passion.

She sighed. "Just don't track dirt in, then. How was your day?" My mom is a nervous woman. She shakes and I can tell she's always trying her hardest. But I still feel like a disappointment to her. I'm not manly. Sometimes, I wondered if it would be better for me to go on some sort of ManQuest and go live out in the wilderness for a month, perhaps kill a bear (or two) in the process. Then she'd never have to be embarrassed at the family reunions when Dad's brothers were bragging about how their sons are the captains of their football teams or dating the head cheerleaders or scoring the most amazing goals in their extracurricular soccer teams.

"Good."

"That's good. Do you need any help with your homework?"

"Mom, I'm not a baby."

"But you're not doing your best. You need to do your best." My mom is obsessed with success. Of course, having a few flaws made me love her. She is human. She is possible. My dad, on the other hand, is too perfect to be believed. He's supportive and loving to the nth degree. It's almost disgusting. I hate it. Luckily, I didn't have to see him too much. He was always traveling.

I went upstairs to my room. My man cave was stuffy, so I opened the window and let the cool air in. My room overlooked the backyard, and there was a huge tree almost devoid of leaves that stood between my house and the house whose backyard mirrored ours.

I fell asleep. A stunted-growing boy needs his rest, after all.

Dinner and night fell. I closed my window.

The next day, Saturday, consisted primarily of my sister hogging the remote.

"Let's watch something better than *The Real Housewives*," I said.

"No. The Atlanta housewives are the best part of my day."

"Then your day is miserable."

"I'm not changing the show."

"I hate you."

"Love you too," she said absently.

Mom came into the family room and stared at me for a second before saying quietly, "Warren? Could you run to the store for me and pick up some carrots for me?"

I was about to argue, but actually I had nothing better to do. I grabbed a jacket and some money from Mom and walked over to the store, which is only about fifteen minutes from our house. I decided to get a twinkie or some other sweet treat to help me lose myself in the utter pain it is to be a geek in the modern age — haha, I love playing the angsty teen.

The grocery bag was light. I zipped up my jacket and stuffed the Ho Ho into my mouth. The air nipped at my nose, and I slouched, as per my natural state. I started walking back home.

It was eerily quiet in suburbia. No one was out doing anything... god, who'd voluntarily move here? For some reason, I've never been able to imagine myself sitting in a cubicle staring at a picture of my wife and two kids waiting to get home to them in our suburban hellhole and play Monopoly. Did I mention that I'm a walking-talking cliché? But besides some generic office work, what else could I do? No drawing skills: I've drawn stick figures that people don't understand are supposed to be people. No writing skills: every essay I've submitted for class has gotten a low B at best. No leadership skills: yeah, just no leadership abilities at all to speak of. No computer skills: despite my pseudo-geek status, I'm not terribly good with computers, just average. My life would be depressing and unremarkable.

I was about three blocks from my house when a suitcase-laden car pulled up beside me and the window slid down. I continued along my way until a gentle voice called out. "Excuse me!"

I stopped and turned to look at the small woman sitting in the front passenger seat of the station wagon. A man, presumably her husband, gripped the steering wheel with white knuckles. "C'mon, Becca. I know how to get there. I've been there before," he whispered. "It's just this goddamn suburbia that's got my senses all messed up." The two girls and one boy in the back snickered. The youngest, a girl with dark blonde hair in pigtails, looked to be about seven. The other two looked about my age.

The wife seemed unperturbed by her husband and smiled at me. "Excuse me, could you tell me where Sakura Street is?"

I thought for a moment; Sakura was the street right past Peachblossom — my street. "Okay, it's actually just two blocks that way." I pointed behind me, to the right of their car.

"Thank you," she said. "These streets all look the same."

"Yeah," I said. I turned promptly away from them and went on my way.

I heard the woman say 'thanks' as they drove past me.

I got home feeling like a good Samaritan for giving directions to strangers. My sister was sitting on the couch with her feet resting on the ottoman, toes wiggling excitedly with their newest coat of bright orange nail polish. She looked up at me. "You look like a turd."

I grinned at her. "Ya think? Is this the right shade of brown?" I asked, unzipping my jacket.

"No," she said. "Can't do anything right, can you? Not even being a turd."

"No, I guess not."

My mom bustled into the room from the kitchen and grabbed the carrots from me. "Thank you." She looked from Lily to me and added, "Be nice to your brother."

Yep, that was exactly what I needed. My mom protecting me, protecting the older brother from the younger sister. She smiled at me, feeling good about herself, though now I felt even less masculine. Thanks, Mom.

I shrugged off the whole situation and ran upstairs, taking it two steps at a time. My room was a tad bit stuffy again, because what man cave isn't? So, I opened my window, letting the snappy chill in. I grabbed my iPod and blasted a little of my angsty geek music, whatever that is — actually, it was just sad pop music with a good beat. Yeah, no rap or metal for me. I fell asleep, because that's what loud noises do to me. They put me to sleep.

My dream wasn't particularly interesting, and I don't remember much of it. Mostly, at the end, I was running through a lollipop forest and a little white bunny with bloodshot eyes bounced up and kicked me in the crotch and shouted at me, "That's for Tibet, bastard."

I jolted awake and shot up into a sitting position. I knew something was funny when I noticed there was a roll of toilet paper in my lap. Actually, getting toilet paper thrown at me was a pretty normal occurrence in my life. It was the fact that it was Charmin Ultra, not Angel Soft, that was out of whack. I yawned and looked around my room for my sister. "C'mon, Lily. Don't be an ass. What kind of joke is this? You're getting less and less funny." No response. "Yeah, at least give me one of your stupid insults, so that I can pretend I don't care."

"Sorry, dude!" said a voice that sounded eerily masculine for being my sister. "I just wanted to check if you were alive. You looked kinda dead sprawled out like that."

I located the owner of the voice. I walked over to my window and gave my best glare at the kid leaning out of the window of the house behind my house.

"Hey, you're the dude that gave us directions."

I squinted at him and focused my eyes. It was the kid — I say kid, but he was about my age — that had been in the backseat of the station wagon with his two sisters, except now he had a pair of binoculars around his neck.

"Are you a creeper?" I asked.

He looked for a second at me with complete confusion. Then he looked down and noticed his binoculars. "Ah, yeah, I guess. Haha, not really."

I was still tired, and that's probably the only reason I was so brotherly. "Don't you dare look at my sister."

I think he grinned — I can't really see that far. "Okay, man." He laughed.

"Did you guys just move in?"

"Yeah."

"Well, you're gonna love this wasteland of human dignity and intelligence."

"Exciting. What school do you go to?"

"Grant. Tenth grade."

"Cool, me and my sister are sophomores, too."

"Are you twins?"

"Yeah."

"Cool, I guess." I tapped the window pane above my head. "Um, I'm gonna go and sleep some more then, okay? Did you need anything?"

He seemed to think for a moment then answered, "Actually, want to hang out with me and my sister tomorrow? We kind of wanted a tour of the town."

I yawned and nodded. "Sure." I shut the window, not intending to fulfill his request. He was a creeper looking for girls to look at with binoculars as soon as he moved in. Even a shut-in geek like me wouldn't consider being so desperate — though, admittedly, since I haven't hit my growth spurt, I haven't been taken over by the raging hormones that accompany adolescence. I pulled the cord to let my blinds fall down over the window; it'd be weird if I knew he could see me. Why did my neighbor have to be a creeper? Now I had to make sure he was not looking at my sister. How was I gonna do that? I can't boast of my physical strength, nor do I boast any great strategical prowess.

I grumbled and thought my way into my second nap. When it was time for dinner, my sister "woke" me by sitting on my stomach. "Wake up, you bastard."

"Shut up, you bitch."

She grinned at me. "You're lucky to have an awesome sister like me."

"Yeah, I always wanted a fat pet alligator. Get off me."

She jumped off me and landed on the carpeted floor with a loud thud. "Dinner's ready." She marched out of my room, but just as she left, she said, "You're a turd. Never call a girl fat."

"I only speak the truth," I lied to empty air.

~

Sunday morning, I woke to my mom barging into my room whispering fiercely about someone at the door. She ripped at the cord to pull up my blinds. I shielded my eyes from light that was not as harsh as I expected.

"I thought he was here for Lily, but he said it was you, Warren. He said he's new and you promised to show him around. Wow, such a handsome boy, maybe I should send Lily with you," Mom said so fast while ripping the covers off my bed.

I groaned. "What are you talking about?" I rubbed my eyes and sat up. "The creepy kid with binoculars?"

Mom ignored me and yanked me out of the bed. "Make sure you talk about your sister."

"What's this? I'm just showing the kid around. I'm not Lily's matchmaker."

Mom giggled. "He's such a handsome boy, Warren. They would be such a cute couple."

I rolled my eyes and pulled on a new shirt and a pair of jeans. "Tell him to wait a few minutes." She left, and I brushed my teeth. I blinked at myself in the mirror and silently swore that this kid took me seriously when I said I'd show him around. Whatever, I said I would, so now I had to.

I spit out the toothpaste and slunk down the stairs. He was standing and looking at our living room. "Hey, man. Where's your sister?"

"She didn't feel like coming."

"Oh, what time is it?"

"Eleven."

I shook my head. "Dude, rule number one: weekends are for sleeping 'til three in the afternoon."

"Sorry," he said, but he was grinning.

I got to the last step and squinted at him. He was probably a foot taller than me — curse tall people, I felt like a hobbit. He was lean and "chiseled" with blonde-ish hair and blue-ish eyes. Haha, chiseled. My mom and sister use that word a lot. "God," I said. "You *are* handsome. By the way, I'm supposed to talk about my sister the whole time." I heard my mom "hmph" from the kitchen. "Love you too, Mom!" It felt good thwarting my mother's devious plans — except they weren't so devious. I turned to the kid. "So, I guess we should go and explore the wonderment that is NorCal. Prepare to have your mind blown." I yanked open the front door and followed him out.

I pointed at my family's lawn. "So," I spoke slowly. "This is grass. Yes, grass. I don't know if they have this where you come from, but here it's the symbol of family and conformity and normalcy. You'll want a lawn if you want to fit in."

"Seems like you've been disillusioned with the American Dream," he said, laughing.

I shrugged. "Me? Naw, I love feeling like I'm a disappointment to my family, because I'm neither sporty nor brainy." I looked up at him. "You play sports, don't you?"

He nodded. "Yeah. And I have a 4.0 GPA, unweighted, of course."

"God, I should pound you to bloody pulp for being everything I should be," I said. "Go all hobbit Kung Fu on your ass. Except it looks like you could lift me up with your little pinkie."

"I probably could." He snickered.

"Go to hell." I started walking in the direction of town. "So, what's your name? Or should I just keep calling you 'kid' in my mind?"

"Call me Kid."

"Okay, Kid. Stop Kidding me and tell me your name," I said, then added, "or I'll beat you up," for good measure.

"I dare you to try."

I rolled my eyes; yeah, it's not that I'm a wimp, I'm just too polite to beat him up during our first meeting and pointed at a tree. "Whatever. That is a tree. They grow really tall, taller than you, Kid. You might think you're superior to me, but the trees are superior to you, and since I have hobbit status, the trees are my domain. That means you are inferior to me."

He laughed.

"Dude, I hate you already."

"Love you too," he said, chuckling.

"Yeah, I'm the lovable neighborhood hobbit." I turned around and walked backwards in front of him. "So, where are you from?"

"Maine."

"East Coast Kid, then. What's it like over there?"

"Colder, greener."

"Real descriptive, Kid."

"Yeah, I should win the Nobel Prize for great oration."

"Yeah, you should. Does one exist for that?"

He shrugged.

We got to the start of our town's commercial district. "And here is your favorite place," I said. "Your greatest moments will be here. After you win the champion football game, your football buddies will carry you on their shoulders all the way to Tally's for an after-game celebration. You'll bring the head cheerleader to a horror movie at Edwards Cinema and eat at that Italian place four streets down. You'll ride in the back of your friend's car, leaning out of the window and shouting nonsense at the top of your lungs after getting totally wasted at Denise's party."

"Wow," he said. "You've pinned me to a T."

I shrugged. "Yeah, I'm good at reading people."

"And what'll you be doing?"

I smiled and shook my head. "My greatest moments won't be here. No, they'll be in my man cave, finally beating *Call of Duty 4*. They'll be when I'm at college, and I'm so desperate for sex that I go so far as to put cocaine in a girl's drink so we can do it, except the drugs won't debilitate her enough to make her wanna do it with me. And that's when I'll attempt to kill myself, but I'll fail. They'll be when I finally get married to some nerd girl who I don't love, but I'll feel like I have to marry, because she's the best I can get." I frowned, because saying it out loud actually made me feel like crying. Wow, my life really will be depressing.

I looked at Kid and tried to smile. "Sorry." I breathed out a long breath and held my shoulders higher, because maybe acting happier would make me happier. "Anyway – "

"Warren!" a voice squeaked.

I turned to look for who it was. Denise, the epitome of the American girl, was there with her ever-present sidekick, Katelyn Freidman. Denise never spoke to me, except that one time two days before when I made her angry. So, naturally, I was flabbergasted that she was smiling at me. "Hi, Denise," I said.

"Who's your friend?" she asked, and suddenly I realized why she was talking to me. Pretty attracts pretty.

I felt very spiteful in that second, so I guess that's why I answered the way I did. "Oh." I put on my most fluttery voice. "This is Kid. He's my long distance boyfriend that I met in Maine last Spring. Isn't he so hot?" I secretly crossed my fingers that Kid wouldn't beat me until I was unrecognizable after this, then wrapped my arm around his waist. Oh, god, he was going to kill me, but I just had to stick it to Denise for even a second.

Her face was priceless.

It was worth it. I closed my eyes, satisfied, and waited for Kid's fist.

Nothing happened. Maybe he was in shock. Maybe I had time to run. But then, I heard Kid say, "Yeah, isn't... Warren just adorable?"

I opened my eyes. It was a miracle... he was playing along.

"I didn't know you were gay," Katelyn said, recovering faster than Denise.

"I didn't know either until I met Kid," I said. I wanted to burst out laughing. It was even better that Kid was playing along.

"Introduce me to your friends, Warren," Kid said. I felt his arm on my shoulder. Man, he was good. It made my skin feel tingly.

"This is Denise Walker," I said. "She's like the most popular girl at our school. And Katelyn Freidman is the star of the soccer team. Girls, this is Kid. He actually just moved here. Isn't it wonderful? I love karma." I smiled, then frowned. "Actually, could you girls keep it on the down low about... us? I mean, people at school will be mean if they knew."

Denise recovered, because she said, "Sure, we wouldn't dream of outing you guys."

"Okay, then, well, we'll see you tomorrow at school," I said, still trying to be as stereotypically gay as I could be.

We walked away, still keeping up the rouse until they were out of sight.

I untangled myself from him and laughed like a hyena. "Dude, I love you. That was awesome! Did you see her face? Oh my god, thank you for playing along. I was sure you were gonna kill me."

He laughed too, though not quite as much as I did, probably because he didn't know what Denise was like.

"Oh my god, that's a story I'm gonna tell my children!" Then I was quiet. "You know she's gonna tell everyone, right?"

"Yeah, that was kinda obvious."

"Oh, sorry, man."

"About what?"

"You had prospects. I kinda just ruined every chance you had of being popular." The thought sobered me up a bit.

"Don't worry, no one'll believe that I'm gay." He laughed. "That was hysterical."

"Yeah," I said, grinning. "And those were the two empty-headed bimbos that have the student body wrapped around their fingers. Better not cross them. Wait, we already did. Slap hands, dude." I held up my hand for a high-five.

He looked at me. "Slap hands?"

I shrugged. "I heard this girl say it once, just high-five." We high-fived. "This is awesome! I can't believe we did that."

We went on our way with me pointing out things that he should know. And I laughed about every ten seconds.

I finished the tour when we got back to my street. "Okay, Kid. Fun hanging with you. Awesome actually!"

"Yeah, ditto."

I walked back to my house and grinned as I entered the house.

"What are you so smiley about?" Lily asked.

"Nothing," I said, implying that there was something but that I wouldn't tell her.

"Mom says he was hot."

"Don't worry," I said. "I made sure that he knew every single one of your bad habits and that you wear underwear with little kangaroos on them."

She glared at me. "Oh, by the way, Denise Walker texted me asking for your number."

I stopped dead. "Did you give it to her?"

"No, because she won't tell me why."

"Haha, okay."

"Why does she want your number?"

"'Cause I'm cool?" I bounded up the stairs to my room with big steps.

~

I gave Denise Walker a little wave when I saw her on Monday morning. She came over to me and whispered, "Is your boyfriend gonna be here today?"

"He said he would be."

Suddenly, Kid was behind me. "Hi, Denise," he whispered. "Hey, Warren. Looking cuter than yesterday, huh?"

I felt goosebumps on the back of my neck, but I grinned. "Hey, Kid."

"Denise, meet my sister Virginia."

I looked at his sister. God, she was a goddess, like the female version of Kid, and, I noted with some excitement, her looks surpassed Denise's. Virginia winked at me and held her hand out to Denise. "Nice to meet you. Glen told me that you're the one to know here."

"Glen?" Denise asked. I wondered who Glen was, too.

"Oh, Glen is Kid's real name. Only Warren calls him Kid." I guess she was in on the ruse, and now I knew Kid's real name.

My first two classes crawled. Katelyn was in my second class with me, and she kept sneaking looks at me. I purposely messed with my hair and pouted my lips when I saw her looking — yes, 'cause that's exactly what gay guys do, trust me.

At brunch, Kid found me and formally introduced me to his twin.

"Virginia, huh? I guess your parents didn't have much Maine state pride."

"Actually, we were born in Virginia," she said.

"Make me eat my words, why don't you?" I turned to Kid and said, "Slap hands." He high-fived.

"You're so short," he said when I had to jump to reach his hand.

"Yeah, don't rub it in. Me 'n my hobbit powers will beat your ass any time, day or night." I held my fist up to him. I stood on my tiptoes, adding about three inches to my sixty-two inch frame.

"Oooh, I'm shivering in my britches," he said and burst out laughing.

"Wanna die, punk?" I asked. I cracked up at the absurdity.

"Get a room, guys," Virginia said.

"Are you homophobic, Virginia?" I asked, joking. "Are you trying to inhibit the blossoming of our love?"

She gave me a look that I didn't understand. "I'll see you guys later. Gotta set out to find my own love prospects."

I turned to Kid. "I like your sister. She's fun. I can't believe she's playing along with it too."

"Yeah."

"We don't have to mess with Denise if you don't want to. If you don't think it's funny, just tell me."

"Naw, it's okay. Show me around the school."

I gave him the abridged tour because the bell rang too soon. Kid was in my fourth class, and when he sat in front of me, I realized that I had made my first friend since elementary school.

It was weird. He was my friend. The knowledge hit me like a brick wall, and I felt giddy. We were friends. Right? Did we need to say it out loud to affirm the fact? How did these types of things work in high school? Did he think we were friends? Well, he sat near me in class, so that was one indication, right? Can being friends happen that fast? We just hung out yesterday. He threw toilet paper at me on Saturday. Can it really be that simple and easy to make friends? If it is, then I'm going to start carrying around five or six toilet paper rolls with me at all times.

I stared at the back of Kid's head and denied it. I couldn't believe that we were friends. We were of a different status. Tall jocks and short geeks just weren't friends. What's the old saying? *Like marry like.* I always thought that applied to friendships too. Like befriends like.

I decided to test whether or not we were friends. If he left the class without me, then he wasn't my friend. Because friends wait for each other after class, right?

The bell rang, and the teacher dismissed us. I put my stuff away slowly, painfully slowly. I looked up just to see Kid walk out with the rest of them. I frowned, crushed. I hadn't made a friend after all.

Mr. Werely, the teacher, stared at me for a second. "Is something wrong?"

I shook my head. "Naw, just slow and tired today." I yawned for added measure.

"If you're not getting enough sleep, you should go see the school nurse. Insomnia is a serious problem."

"Mr. Werely, I'm fine," I said, irritated. He was one of those teachers that felt the need to be ultra compassionate and understanding, and sometimes it was hard handling his utter altruism with good humor. "I'll see you tomorrow, Mr. Werely."

"Okay, Warren. See you tomorrow."

I slung my backpack over my shoulder and hurried out of the room.

Kid was standing right there next to the door. I was surprised. That meant he was my friend, right?

"So, what's the best food in the cafeteria?"

I thought for a moment, then answered, "The burritos, definitely."

"Let's get some then. I'm gonna die of starvation."

We each bought a bean and cheese burrito from the fat lady running the food cart outside the cafeteria.

~

Friday, after fourth period, when we were walking down to the cafeteria to get some food, Kid turned to me and said, "Hey, I need to go get some clothes today. Want to show me the mall?"

I grinned. We were going to hang out outside of

school; friends did that. "Sure, but you know that malls are the breeding grounds for blonde zombies and little Chihuahua dogs who shiver at the slightest wind, right?"

"I know."

"You're already halfway to being a blonde zombie. I mean, look at your hair."

He pulled a chunk of his hair so that he could see it. "You're right. I've gotta be careful."

"Yeah."

After school, we met up at the school's flag pole. Man, he was tall. It made me feel more unusually small when I looked at him.

I led the way to the mall. "Dude, were you held back a grade or two?"

"What?"

"Did they feed you steroids when you were a baby?"

"Hmm?"

"How'd you get so goddamned tall?"

He shrugged.

I elbowed him hard in the stomach. "I hate you."

He grinned. "Love you too."

Then I monologued because Kid doesn't say that much, and I like to talk about the amazing graphics of *Call of Duty 4.*

The mall was busy. The shopping portion of our trip was short. Kid was very no-nonsense about the whole deal. I'd sit in some chair at the store, and he'd pick out something, try it on and buy it or put it back. It was refreshing compared to the few times I've been to the mall with my sister and she agonizes over the decision and ends up buying nothing.

Finally, Kid finished at the register in our last store, and he sighed and smiled. "Okay, sorry for taking so long, but my mom said I had to get something nice to wear. We're going to some family thing tomorrow."

I nodded and stood up. "I'm hungry. Buy me food as compensation for all of my time that you wasted."

He frowned. "Okay – "

I grinned. "Dude, you're a pushover. Let's go."

We each bought our own food at the Panda Express in the food court. I looked at my orange chicken while my mouth watered. Patience. Wait a few seconds longer, the wait makes it better. Screw waiting. I ate like a pig. I looked up at Kid. He had this vacant look in his eyes.

What? Did I need to have manners? Was he picky about stuff like that? Were friends not allowed to eat like pigs in front of each other? Maybe we weren't friends then. I stopped eating. He kept looking. Maybe it wasn't me. I turned around and saw Denise and Katelyn sitting at their own table.

He liked Denise then. Why else would he stare at her?

"Hey, dude. Why don't you go talk to her? Just tell her I was messing with her," I said, being the altruistic friend that I am. "Tell her we were joking."

His eyes narrowed. "Huh?"

"You like Denise, right? You're staring at her like a lost little puppy."

"Denise?"

"Yeah, I saw her behind me. You were staring."

He shook his head. "I wasn't staring at her."

"Katelyn, then?"

"No."

I frowned. "Don't tell me that you were grossed out by my eating."

He grinned.

"Man, I didn't know you were an etiquette Nazi." I laughed and stuck a huge piece of orange chicken into my mouth. I tried to chew as disgustingly as I could manage.

He chuckled, but I grossed him out enough that he had to look away after a while. "I win," I said, swallowing.

He shook his head. "No, I just thought I saw a penny on the floor. You stopped. I win."

~

Sunday — after 3 P.M. of course, rule number one — Kid knocked on my door. We hung out in my room playing *Call of Duty 4*. Lily kept sneaking looks at Kid whenever she walked past my door, and she found lots of reasons to walk past.

Finally, I yelled for her to come in.

She was blushing. "Hi," she said to Kid.

He barely took his eyes off the TV screen. Playing hard to get. "Hi, Lily. My sister says you're cool."

"Thanks." Lily sat down next to me on my bed.

"How's cheerleading going?"

"Good."

"Is Virginia being nice to you?"

Lily turned to me. "Yeah. She's lots of fun."

"Good." Kid turned to me. "That's good." The corner of his mouth rose and then he put his attention back on the TV.

Lily left.

Two weeks passed, and I felt like we were friends for real, though neither of us had said it. Maybe you don't have to say it. It was colder now. Mom had started putting up Christmas decorations. Holiday music was playing on the radio. School only had three weeks before Winter Break.

We were walking to the tables chomping down on burgers that we bought from the skinny lady inside the cafeteria, and I was asking Kid which sport was his favorite, when Denise and Katelyn sauntered up to us.

I smirked and elbowed Kid. "This is gonna be hysterical."

He nodded, not taking his eyes off Denise.

"Hi, Glen. Hi, Warren."

"Hey," Kid and I said together.

"So, me 'n Katelyn are throwing a party this Friday, and we wanted to invite you guys. You guys can come together and everything. We're totally chill with that."

"Really?" I said. "Why invite me?"

She shrugged.

"You've never invited me before." I raised an eyebrow at her.

"Never thought of inviting you before. So are you gonna come?"

"I'll come," I said. "If Kid wants to go." I looked up at him, and he smiled.

"Sure, we'll come," he said slowly. I wondered if there was something he was thinking, perhaps a devious plan that I wanted to take part in.

"Great," Denise said, clapping her hands together. She turned to Katelyn and said, "Give them an invitation." She smiled up at Kid and said, "Well, see you there." The two girls turned on their heels and marched off.

Kid chuckled and looked at me. "She's onto us."

"Really?" I asked. "I thought I was doing a bang up job if I do say so myself." I looked at him. "We should stop then, huh? You like her, don't you?"

"Huh?"

"You like her, right?"

"Denise?"

"Yeah, I saw you looking at her," I said. "You don't have to keep up the ruse if you like her. Just because she's my imaginary arch nemesis doesn't mean she has to be yours. Actually it's kind of sad that the only one I feel is my nemesis is a girl. Not a football jock like you."

He shook his head, smiling. "I don't like her." He put his hand on my shoulder. "Trust me, I don't like her. Plus, it's gonna be funny when she's humiliated."

"Okay, just making sure."

When I got home that day, Lily was waiting for me. "How come she invited you and not me?" she screamed.

It took me a moment to register what she was talking about. "Denise's party?"

"YEAH, HER PARTY, YOU GODDAMN BAS-TARD. Why?"

I shrugged. "Because I'm cool like that?"

She shook her head. "No, that's not it."

"So, you agree that I'm cool?"

"NO!"

"Maybe she's fallen madly in love with me?"

"Ew, definitely not."

"'Cause I'm besties with a tall, dark and hand-some hottie?" I suggested in the most annoying voice I could conjure up, mostly I was mimicking the way Lily would talk. I think my diction was suitable.

"What?" Her voice broke. She had no clue what I was talking about, and she was just getting more frus-trated.

I sighed. She was upset, not just angry. "She only invited me to get close to Kid."

She straightened up and said, "Oh." She smiled. "Thank you." She slammed the door to my room.

I sighed and felt miserable that the only reason someone would invite me to their party was because of the way my friend looked. I didn't even feel like going anymore. I surveyed my room and it was a mess, just like my social life. A week-old sandwich on my desk. A pile of dirty clothes on my window seat. Game controllers sprawled on the floor with the oc-casional popcorn kernel imbedded in the carpet. My bed wasn't made. I didn't even dare look in the general direction of my closet. Papers were scattered just about everywhere.

My neck lost all its strength, and my head fell. "God." I lay on my bed and went to sleep. I think that's my default, sleeping.

~

I got to Thursday before I broke. I just wanted to make sure, and I didn't think I'd get the answer I got. After our fourth period together, I craned my neck to see Kid's face and asked, "Hey, I know this is kind of a weird question, but are we friends?"

He didn't answer at first, so I started to blab. "It's not a big deal or anything. It's just I'm not sure, y'know. Is it inappropriate to think we're friends? I mean, do you consider us friends?"

He frowned and slowly answered, "No. I don't consider us friends."

"Oh, okay," I said, but I was cursing his grand-children in my mind. "Well, thanks for the fun, then." Damn them all to hell. Curse you, Kid Junior and Kid the Third. I walked away. Of all the answers he had to give me, he had to just flat out say no? Man, what an idiot. He could have been polite and said sure. He could have thought of some other way to not completely crush my spirit. Does he have no soul?

By the end of lunch, I was done being melodra-matic in my mind. Not once did I blame myself for asking in the first place, because in this day and age, who ever turns their criticism inward? I certainly was not going to be the first.

I walked home by myself, like usual, and smiled glumly at my sister when she got home from cheerleading practice. "Well, turns out me 'n Kid aren't friends. So, you can rejoice."

Her eyebrows snapped together. "I'm not as evil as you think."

"And the sky isn't blue."

"Whatever." She dropped her bag and took the remote control out of my hand. "It's my turn to pick the show." She fell on top of me and giggled. She banged her head against my stomach.

"I hate you," I told her, after I could breathe again.

"Love you too, loser." She switched through the channels and settled on an episode of *MTV Cribs*.

Tears of pain fell from my eyes as I watched some baseball player show me his wife's three shoe closets. "Oh, c'mon, Lily. Turn something else on. This is painful to watch. I'm gonna turn into a mindless zombie."

She grinned up at me. "My evil plan is coming to fruition." She laughed.

I pouted. "Please, pretty please with a cherry on top?"

She rolled her eyes. "What do you want to watch?"

"TV Land?"

"No."

"History Channel?"

She shook her head.

"Sy-Fy?" By the way, I hate the new spelling.

No, again.

"Lifetime?"

"Okay." She switched, and we watched *Drop Dead Diva*, which was admittedly better than *MTV Cribs* — by a hair, I swear, by a hair.

When Lily fell asleep, I pushed her off me and went to the kitchen for a snack. My mom was on her computer chatting to her college friends on the east coast; it was surprising that she wasn't cleaning. She turned around and smiled at me. "Want something to eat, sweetie?"

"Yeah," I said. "But I'll make it myself."

"Your dad is coming home on Monday."

"That'll be fun."

"Yeah, we miss him."

"Yeah, we do." I pulled open the fridge and looked inside. Everything was meticulously clean and organized. Mom must have OCD. I grabbed a water bottle — all you environmentalists out there, kiss my ass — and a hunk of Hungarian sausage — you too, you vegetarians. Naw, JK, JK, Warren loves you all, he just be angsty — how's that for annoying third person?

I went back and watched *Drop Dead Diva*. Lily still slept. Her mouth was open, and she snored quietly.

I got a text from Kid, which was weird, because I never gave him my number. *Hey, it's Kid. I think you misunderstood me.*

I ripped off a chunk of my meat and chewed and replied, *Nothing to misunderstand. You don't want to be friends. I understand completely.*

I had just taken a swig of my water when I got a reply. *I was right; you misunderstood me.*

I glared at my phone like he could feel my wrath, though I don't know why I was so mad. I mean, three weeks, less than that. I guess because I hadn't had a friend in so long that I grew attached so quickly. *It doesn't matter. You said it yourself. You don't consider me a friend, so that means we can't be friends if the both of us don't agree on that. Well, sorry for misunderstanding. And don't look at my sister with those binoculars of yours.* I smirked.

He didn't reply anymore.

I forced myself to smile.

"You look dumb."

I closed my eyes. She was awake. "Well, you snore like a chainsaw."

"That was the worst comeback I've ever heard."

"You ate a spider when you were sleeping."

"You're gay."

"You're fat."

"You're a wimp."

"You're a bitch."

"You're a bastard, and if you say anything more, I'm gonna switch back to *MTV Cribs*."

You're ugly, I countered in mind. I ate my meat and watched the fat woman — no, I'm not judgmental at all — on the TV realize that by being stuck in her new body, she has lost eight years of her life. I wondered how it felt to be that woman. It would be really terrible if I was suddenly twenty three, and I had nothing to show for it. It made me want to go and do my homework, but I didn't get up. I just kept watching.

After three episodes of *Drop Dead Diva*, I yawned and told Lily that she could watch whatever she wanted. I trudged to my room and cracked open my math book. I finished that homework and read my English assignment and started my Chemistry before losing all hope and succumbing to sleep.

~

Friday morning, I woke without my mom ripping my blanket off me. My eyes just opened, and I couldn't sleep anymore. I stared at my unset alarm clock. It was 5:49 am. The sun wasn't even out yet.

I went and took a shower. The water washed away nothing of yesterday. I was still utterly devastated that my first friend in years turned out not to be my friend. But I did feel squeaky clean. I wrapped a towel around me and went back to my room.

I almost dropped my towel when I saw Kid sitting at his window. He was looking for my sister, again? I marched over to my window and opened it and yell-whispered, "Dude, didn't I tell you not to look at my sister?"

His eyes seemed to shoot needles right into my soul, and I shot him my most piercing look in return, though

I'm sure it wasn't as effective as his. Who could compete with a face like his? "I'm not looking at your sister."

"Yeah, and the sky isn't blue."

He looked up, and a smile stretched across his face. "Actually, right now, it's gray."

"You know what I mean."

"So, when do I come and pick you up tonight?"

"What?"

"For Denise's party?"

"We're not friends, so there's no need. Go by yourself and just tell 'em we were joking."

"I just said that we're not friends. That doesn't mean we can't be friendly."

"That doesn't make sense at all. If we're not friends, how can we be friendly?"

He shrugged. "Think about it."

I shook my head. "No." And I shut my window. I grabbed my clothes and went to a part of my room where the window had no view of me and got dressed. I grabbed my school bag and went downstairs. My mom was dusting the staircase. When she saw me, she smiled. "Hi, honey."

"Hi, Mom."

"Is something wrong?"

"No, I'm just going to go to school early."

"Okay, be safe."

"I will." I grabbed an orange from the kitchen and headed out the door.

I was about a block from my house when a hand grabbed my arm.

"Okay, Warren. If you really don't get what I'm saying, then let's just be friends the way you think we should be," Kid said. He scratched the back of his head, looking at the ground. "Maybe I was wrong in assuming what I did."

"If you assume, you make an ass out of you and me," I said, still not getting what he was saying. God, this Kid was cryptic, but I laughed to show him my good will.

He smiled at me. "I guess I did." He laughed, though he didn't seem quite happy. "Can you wait for me? I need to grab my stuff. I didn't know you were going to school."

"I'll wait, but first let me give you the second rule if we're gonna be friends: don't pull that friendly crap on me. I can't take it."

He bit his upper lip and said, "Okay. I won't say anything about it anymore."

"'Kay," I chirped. "I'll wait right here."

He didn't say another word and just ran off. He was back before I knew it.

On our walk to school, I did my best to pretend that the previous day hadn't happened. "So, how's suburbia treatin' you, Kid? Fallen in love with the cookie cutter street names and cookie cutter people?"

"Yeah, I'm madly in love."

"Good, good. It's simply devastating when there isn't love in the world," I said. Man, I wasn't on my game today.

"Yeah."

"You have any rules for me?"

"What?"

"I've already given you two rules for our friendship. One: don't wake me up before 3 P.M. on a weekend. Two: no friendly crap. Do you have any for me?" I asked. "I don't want to be bossy."

"No, I don't have any rules."

I laughed. "Good, I wasn't going to follow your rules anyway."

He frowned. "Are we still gonna go to her party?"

"Well, if you don't mind, I think it'd be awesome to mess with her some more. Oh, you can see it in her eyes that she wants you so bad." The wind blew hard suddenly, and I wrapped my jacket tighter around me. "Damn, it's cold."

"You want my jacket?"

"Huh?" I turned to him and shook my head. "No, I've got to rough it out and be a man. Thanks, though...y'know, this is the beginning of a beautiful friendship."

"How so?"

"Well, I mean, I make up the rules and order you around, and you offer me your jacket when I'm cold? Dude, you're the best friend I've ever had. Well, actually, that's not much competition seeing as I've only had one other friend, and he moved away in fourth grade. Still, you take the cake."

"Thanks, I guess."

"Don't worry, Kid. I won't take advantage of you and your kindness. I just like marveling in the fact that I actually have a friend. Just tell me if you need anything."

"Okay."

We got to school extraordinarily early. The gate hadn't even been unlocked yet.

I sat and leaned against the school wall, but Kid just paced. "Hey, Kiddo. Is something wrong?"

He stopped, stared at me for a second, and shook his head. "No, just thinking."

"Penny for your thoughts?"

"Haha, no."

"Oh, you're mean."

"You wouldn't want to know my thoughts right now."

"Why not?"

"I'm breaking rule number two."

"Oh." I didn't quite know what he meant, but let it slide because I was in a good mood. I stared at Kid as he arched his back, reached up and plucked a pine needle off a tree. I know this sounds so weird, but it was supremely beautiful. It was like dance had been boiled down to its simplest form. I've seen *So You Think You Can Dance* a few times. And sometimes, a dancer just moves, and I feel like I'm at a museum staring at the *Mona Lisa* or *Starry Night*. That was the first moment that I ever saw something in real life that gave me that feeling. I didn't say anything, of course. Who would ever say something so cheesy out loud? Instead, I ruined the momentary serenity in my mind and blurted out, "So, your sister's hot." As soon as I said it, I felt like

I had betrayed the beauty of the movement with something meaningless.

He turned to me slowly and smiled, but the smile seemed watery. "Yeah, I guess she would be considered that. You like her?"

I didn't expect him to turn it on me, but I thought about it for a moment. "No, I don't think I do." I chuckled. "You'd think I'd like her, right? I mean, she's absolutely gorgeous, if you don't mind me saying." I shrugged. "Raging teenage hormones haven't taken over my body, I guess."

His eyes brightened.

"That's the spirit. Turn that frown upside-down."

He proceeded to demolish the pine needle in a methodical sort of way, ignoring what I said.

"Yeah, take out whatever inner rage you have on that poor defenseless piece of foliage."

"Rage?"

"Yeah, you're obviously upset about something." I clasped my hands together and fluttered my eyes. "Won't you tell me?"

"No."

"Fine then." I crossed my arms over my chest in mock-irritation. "Be that way."

"Y'know that you don't make any sense, right?"

"Why, thank you. I take pride in my randomness."

We talked about nothing in particular, waiting for a janitor to unlock the gate. When we got inside the school, I told Kid that I actually didn't have anything to really study, but I asked him to "help" me with my

Chem — the scare quotes around *help* are because when people help you, most of the times they just give you the answer.

The day passed relatively quickly. Kid and I walked home and roared with laughter about our plan. The plan even included a fake kiss! It was going to be golden, for sure.

Now, some might feel inclined to say that I was gay for going to such an extent. But come on. If someone who never talked to you came up and talked to you because the guy standing next to you could be considered a god, you'd of course have to pretend to be gay, just to make her feel bad because she couldn't have him. Wow, that does actually sound kinda gay, but trust me, it's not. I just don't like Denise and since Kid doesn't like her either — though I'm not exactly sure about this. Isn't it awesome that we can rub it in her face the fact that she won't get Kid?... I'm digging my hole deeper, aren't I?

Well, whatever. It makes sense to me. Plus, Kid doesn't seem to have a problem with it.

The next evening, Kid and I met at the corner of my street at seven thirty. "Slap hands, man."

"This is gonna make her jaw drop." Kid high-fived me.

"I know. By the way, I just want to make sure you still wanna do it. 'Cause y'know. No one thinks of me as a man, so I've got no reputation to ruin. You, on the other hand, are like...y'know."

He shrugged. "I'm game."

I grinned at him. "Hey, you know what's funny?" Kid waited for me to elaborate. "Okay, I started thinking about it, and the fact that we're pretending to be gay sounds pretty gay to begin with. I mean, what two straight guys have the cojones to pretend to be gay? You're a real man, Kid."

"Yeah," he smirked. "Let's go."

We got to a block from Denise's house, and I stopped. "How're we gonna do this?" I asked, then chuckled, because the idea of us holding hands was so preposterous. I held out my hand and tried to keep from cracking up.

He raised his eyebrows at me, shook his head and snickered. He grabbed my hand.

"Your hand is very soft," I said, joking, but genuinely surprised. "Are you metrosexual?"

"Uh, sure, why not. Thanks, though. Your hand is, uh, small."

I nodded vigorously. "Uh huh. Like a girl's, right?" Words just piled out of my mouth sometimes. I couldn't control it.

He shrugged. "I guess, not really."

I stared up at the sky and breathed in a sharp breath. "Sorry, gay people out there. What we do is for comedy... and some spite."

"Yeah, sorry."

I giggled like a schoolgirl then, because man, who wouldn't?

We walked the last block slowly. I wondered if maybe Kid wanted to back out. I might've if my manhood was on the line, but I had apparently lost that a long time ago.

"Oh my god, you really are gay." I turned, still holding Kid's hand, to face my accuser. Some random cheerleader whose name I was vaguely aware of.

I nodded.

"Well," she said. "I always thought you were gay, Warren. But I didn't believe it when Katelyn said you were gay, Glen. What a waste."

"Isn't it amazing that I bagged such a hottie?" I asked, channeling my sister.

She actually agreed with me. Isn't it polite to never let the person you're talking to know that you think they're ugly? God, so rude.

She winked at Kid and said, "If you ever turn or anything, I'm available." She made her excuses and ran ahead of us.

I looked at Kid. "Wow, man, she wasn't subtle at all." I actually felt a tad of hurt. I mean, if we had actually been dating, she basically tried to steal my "man" in broad daylight and called me homely in the process. "Vicious."

There weren't a lot of people at the party since it was so early, but every single one of them came up and talked to us — well the girls at least. We went to Denise's kitchen, which was sparkling, and looked over the spread.

The chips were in a crystal bowl, as was the dip. The prepackaged finger food had been removed from their plastic homes and arranged artfully on actual platters. One thing that let me feel as if the world was right again was the red plastic cups towered next to the two-liter plastic bottles of soda. No beer — and being the goody two-shoes that I am I wouldn't have drunk any anyways, probably — but I was sure someone else would be bringing some. Well, maybe, what the hell do I know? I've never been invited to this kind of shindig before.

We let go of our hands, and I ate like a starving rat. Kid still keeping up the ruse — what an actor — poured soda for me and himself.

The party was just getting warmed up in the other room. The Katy Perry song about being a lesbian came on, and I saw something that made me swallow my half-chewed sour cream-laden chip. I winked at Kid and grabbed his shirt and pulled him closer. "Best boyfriend ever." Then I got up on my tiptoes and whispered in his ear, "Denise is watching."

Kid's eyes snapped to attention, but thankfully he remembered not to turn and look at her. He suddenly had his arms on either side of me, as per our plan, gripping the counter. I stood on my toes again, so he wouldn't have to duck his head so far.

He brought his face so close to mine that I felt hot. He grinned sheepishly at me. "Sorry." After a second or two, I slowly moved my hands to the back of his neck.

My stomach didn't feel so well, maybe the sour cream had been bad, but I forced a silent laugh. "I can feel her death rays penetrating the air."

"Is this long enough?"

"No, just a moment longer. If it's too short, she'll be suspicious."

He did as I said and then leaned back. I felt the blood rushing to my face and checked his face. He was bright red. That made me feel better, because if a manly man like him was perturbed by it, it was okay that I was too. I slid my hands from his neck and sarcastically gushed, "Dude, you're an amazing kisser." We hadn't actually kissed, but part of me suddenly wanted to find out if he was. Though, hell if I know what a good kiss was from any other quality of kiss.

He snorted. "Thanks, I try."

I snuck a look at Denise, and she looked heartbroken. I grabbed my soda off the counter. "Let's go say 'hi' to Denise." Before I started to walk, I remembered the fake romance and snatched up Kid's hand.

"Enjoying the party?" Denise asked. Not one to ever let on that she's flustered, her mouth was plastered with a huge smile.

"It's awesome," I said. I lifted the hand that held Kid's. "It's so wonderful that you invited us together. Nice to see that someone is understanding of our *relationship.*"

Her shoulders collapsed a little, but she flipped her hair ever so slightly and giggled. "No worries."

"Um, we actually have a date after this. So, would you mind if we left early?"

"Sure, it was terrific that you came!"

"Thanks again for inviting us," Kid added before yanking me toward the door.

I could hardly contain my joy before we got out of the neighborhood. "Freakin' sweet!" I shrieked. I ripped away from him and laughed with my eyes on the sky. "Funniest crap in the world!"

~

Monday morning the school was abuzz with talk about our "kiss." Girls who had never even acknowledged my existence waved at me. Guys, who have never talked to me anyway, didn't talk to me.

It surprised me how many people knew. Denise and Katelyn must have been glued to their phones all weekend.

Russell Jonson said hi to me like usual.

"Hey," I said, surprised that he was talking to me. I mean, no guys were talking to me at all. It was like they thought gay was contagious. Maybe Russell hadn't heard.

"So, I heard about the infamous kiss." Nevermind, he knew, and he was talking about it.

"Yeah," I said. "Who knew it'd be such a big deal?"

Russell nodded. "So, see you around, I guess."

"Bye."

When I saw Kid, we slapped hands, and we grinned like fools.

One confused and out-of-the-loop senior guy came up to us and actually asked what was going on. I winked at him and did my best Lily-giggle. "I'm not telling."

When he went and asked someone else, he turned back to me and looked like he was going to cry, because I supposedly flirted with him; hahahaha, the supreme power I now hold.

"This is hysterical, isn't it?" I asked Kid.

"Yeah." He didn't seem as enthused as I was, but I ignored it.

When my sister came home that afternoon, her face was stretched into the biggest smile I'd ever seen. "I knew it," she said.

I cocked my head to the side and let her think whatever she wanted. "TV's mine." I grabbed the remote and ignored her.

It was funny, because she plopped next to me on the couch and didn't say a word more. We watched in silence. I didn't move, because it was like a miracle she hadn't said anything remotely mean and I felt like movement would ruin our peace.

Some random host on the TV introduced the game show contestants. The first, a well-endowed housewife from Wisconsin, bounced into her assigned place for the game. The second, a hard-looking businessman from LA, sauntered to his space. The last, a young aspiring dancer from Tennessee, hopped onto her spot. They were competing for a thousand bucks with a series of spelling challenges. I thought the man would win — because I'm sexist — but it turned out that the blonde and booby housewife triumphed. She did her blonde dance, which basically consisted of a lot of frivolous shaking and bouncing.

I couldn't help but smile.

"Is Kid that awesome?" Lily asked.

I frowned and turned to her and shrugged. A smile crept over my face. "Yeah. Yeah, he is."

Her fingers tightened on the couch. She sighed. "You're so lucky. I wish I could find such an awesome guy like that."

My stomach swelled, because even though it was fake, she considered it real. Her reality projected itself onto mine, and for a second, I considered myself to be lucky. Funny how gay that sounds, but just trust me, any straight guy would feel the same way.

We watched the Game Show Network for a long time, until I finally heard my dad's taxi pull into the driveway. Time seemed to slow down then — yeah, slow-mo isn't just a cinematic creation, it is a natural phenomenon.

There was the sound of a key being inserted into the lock. Lily and I both watched the door handle turn. He came in.

My sister sprang up and squealed. "Daddy, you're home!" She put her long legs to work and leapt onto him like a monkey. Mom bustled in, and she looked so happy. "Honey, we've missed you!"

Dad roared with laughter and spun Lily around. While Lily still hung on him, he pecked Mom's lips, grinning like he'd just had his first drink of water in years. I stared at them and didn't move.

My dad is like a one of those statues of the Greek gods. Beautiful is the only way to describe him. Tall, so tall. Fit, so amazingly fit for a man who spent all his hours in the office. Wonderful, so wonderful a man that he denies what he wants most — to spend time with his family — so he can support his family. Perfect, in every way imaginable. Star of the football team in high school and college. Perfect GPA. Extracurriculars up the wazoo.

God, and I have to live up to that? I stood and grinned up at Dad. He grinned back and swallowed me in a bear hug.

You want to know the worst thing about having the perfect dad? I can't fault him for anything. I can't blame him, because he has loved me wholly and provided everything for me. He's not one of those distant estranged fathers. He's there, and he's involved as much as he can be considering his job. He's never hypocritical and never short-tempered. Kids with druggie dads or absent fathers are screaming at me now, but you don't understand. You will never understand. You can blame your dad. I can't. He didn't spoil me and he didn't ever judge me. He knows everything before I tell him — and when I wanted to impress him in second grade with my new knowledge about mosquitoes, he pretended to have no clue to make me feel better, but it was obvious he knew everything there was to know about mosquitoes and everything else I've ever talked about — and he can do every single thing better than me. And he's such a great father that he doesn't even rub it in my face. He messes up on purpose when we race or build something or have some sort of competition just to be considerate. So, I can't even fault him for being inconsiderate.

I know this just sounds so weird, but growing up is about finding what you're good at, but I can't do that, because he's better than me at every single thing. See, my mom is fine. She's like OCD or something, and she wishes that I would be better — and my dad wishes I was better too, but it is a wholly different variation of wish, because Dad doesn't wish it for his sake but for my sake.

And all I am is an angsty teenager who "hates" the world and only finds joy in messing with the head cheerleader. Can you tell that I'm just a tiny bit bitter? See? And the bitterness is all my fault, too, which makes it doubly worse.

"Is anything wrong, Warren?" he asked, and I could've punched him for being so intuitive.

I shook my head, acting like I had no clue how he had reached that conclusion.

Then, Lily giggled. "Nothing wrong at all, Dad." It took me a second to realize what she meant. She was going to tell him about Kid and me, because she was under the impression that I was gay.

I gave her my most scary *you-better-not-tell-him* glare, but she just turned away from me. She was going to tell him, whether I liked it or not. I wondered how he would react. He wasn't ridiculously religious, and he had never gave an inkling that he had anything against the gays — he has nothing against anyone, except maybe child molesters. But I secretly wished that he'd be completely obliterated, like maybe I'd found his weakness. I clenched my stomach and waited.

"But guess what?" Lily asked. I suppose I could've still stopped her. Shout out some meaningless thing, but it didn't occur to me.

"What?" Dad asked in return. *Don't say it. Don't say it*, I thought furiously, but didn't move. I don't know why it bothered me so much. It was fake-dating; I could easily deny it.

"Warren has a boyfriend."

I studied Dad for a flicker of dislike, an unseeable flinch. Something. A sign that my dad wasn't as perfect as I thought he was. But, no. He didn't miss a beat, like he knew the whole time. He grinned at me. "Well, congratulations. Is he cute?"

I felt like crying. Nothing I could do made my dad waiver in the slightest in his love and devotion. I did find some comfort in looking at Mom though. She looked like a terrified bird, her eyes flitting about like they were on fire. I saw her hands shake just a tad before she remembered herself. Mom tries to be perfect like Dad, but she can't measure up in the least. It's what makes her so endearing, though. She tries so hard. I smiled at her. She smiled back.

"Oh, god, Dad! This kid is like the hottest boy I've ever seen! I mean, drool-worthy, for sure. He's like as tall as you and chiseled – " there it is, that word! " – like he was made by the hands of Michelangelo himself. And as far as I can tell he's like the nicest guy ever!"

I smirked. "Sounds like you're jealous." I guess I should've denied that it was true, but for some reason I didn't. It's easy to play along with a lie, easier than I thought with people I love.

"Why are all the hot guys taken or gay?" she asked in a forlorn sort of way.

I snorted. "You're fourteen, and you've only been in contact with probably a handful of hot guys. How do you know?"

"I know." She shot me a look that was full of deadly intent and then she was all smiles when she turned back to Dad. "So, Daddy, how long are you home this time?"

His face really lit up. "I've got a whole month at the local office."

Lily squealed. "We're gonna have so much FUN!"

~

Tuesday, Dad insisted that I invite Kid over.

After fourth period while Kid was devouring his burrito, I put on my sweetest, most innocent smile on — I wonder how sweet and innocent a fifteen-year-old boy can look but whatever. It was weird trying to start off. "Hey, Kid... so... yeah."

"Hmm?" His eyebrows rose in question.

"So, guess what?"

He held up a hand and swallowed. "What?"

"My dad is back from China!"

"Your dad was in China?"

"Yeah, he's works over there most of the time."

"Oh, that's cool. Is it nice have him back?"

It actually took me a second to answer. "Yeah, it is."

He shrugged. "Cool, then."

"So, he kind of thinks I'm gay and that we're dating for real," I said. The blood flooded my face, and I looked away. He was probably questioning if I really was gay; it was so embarrassing. "See," I paused. "The thing is that my sister heard it from everyone else at school, and she kind of told him. And I didn't deny it, because... he seemed genuinely excited, y'know? So, could you come over today and kind of pretend with me?" My stomach hurt and I waited for the barrage of accusations.

But to my surprise, he shrugged — man, he shrugs a lot. "Sure, I guess." Then he frowned.

"If you don't want to, it's fine. I'll just tell him you're busy or somethi – "

"No, no." He shook his head. "It's fine, but could you wait for me after school? I've got a special tryout for the football team, and yeah. The coach said that this is my only chance, since he already held tryouts for next year's team a month ago."

"Sure, sure, that's fine. I'll wait." My chest tightened. "Is it weird that I didn't deny it?" my voice barely squeaked out.

He looked me straight in the eyes and then his mouth hardened. He shook his head. "No, it isn't," his voice was strained.

We stared at each other for a long moment. I

knew he was just saying that to make me feel better; he thought I was gay for sure. I knew it, and he'd find a reason to not be friends soon enough. I know that me knowing this so intuitively when I've only had one other friend sounds preposterous, but I knew, I knew. My neck ached with the realization.

Thank god Virginia came up to us at precisely that moment. She chuckled and asked, "So, are you guys having a moment or something?"

I glared at her and refused to acknowledge her comment. "Did you know Kid is trying out for the football team?"

She gave me a look like I was an idiot. "He's my twin. I know everything there is to know about him."

Kid laughed. "Yeah, now you do. What about before last year?"

She groaned. "That was 'cause you were keeping it from me."

"What? Tell me," I said. My ears pricked with excitement.

Kid stopped laughing and looked at me seriously. "You don't need to know."

Wow, I almost choked on my own spit. That look gave me a chill so bad that I involuntarily shivered. Guess I never want to be on his bad side. Something terrifying had flashed in his eyes, and I didn't say a word more.

When the final bell rang that afternoon, I made my way down to the football field. I hung back at the side of the bleachers and watched Kid shake hands with

Coach Carr. The team wasn't out there yet, so I assumed that they weren't practicing today.

Until, that is, terror seized up my limbs. They didn't even have to say anything for me to turn around.

Three of the most buff football guys at our school stood around me — why is it always three?

The one in the middle, Jared, started off. "So, you're a fag."

I didn't deny it. This would have been the perfect time to, I'm sure. But maybe it was because if I was going to pretend to be gay, I couldn't just pretend when it was convenient for me — you can tell I'm an actor at heart, a method actor of course. I grinned at them and said, "If you touch me, that means you want my gay cooties. Did you know that I was turned gay because this guy at Vons brushed past me and wham-o, gay?!"

They hesitated. I can't believe they hesitated! God, maybe I should've told them I had AIDS — sorry, people with AIDS, I don't mean to make light of your condition.

"We're not idiots," Jared countered.

"Oooh, I can't believe you still want to touch me. You want to touch a boy." I nodded at the other two and pointed at Jared — incognito, of course. "Someone here is gay," I whispered. "And I'm not talking about me."

I pushed Jared too far, and suddenly he had dragged me three feet by the collar of my shirt. I squeezed my eyes shut tight and covered my face — though I'm not really sure why, but even a geek has to keep up the pretense that he indeed has a face worth protecting.

"Guys," said a voice that was more bored than anything. "C'mon."

No blows yet. Maybe, whoever it was had some power over these guys, but I felt my shirt being pulled again. For a long moment, there was nothing, and I was crushed that my would-be savior had ditched me. But goodness prevailed. "Leave him alone."

The tension on my shirt lessened, and I opened my eyes.

God, I had to really strain my neck more than usual to get a look at my protector. Richard Fletcher. Captain of the football team, and god, a true giant — a gentle giant, might I add, if that doesn't seem too gay? Standing next to most guys at my school, my five feet and two inches made me look small. Next to Kid, I looked like a kid. But next to Richard, I achieved true hobbit status. This guy was for sure scouted by every basketball team from here to Timbuktu — can't believe he chose football instead.

"Get to practice," Richard ordered, and Jared wavered for a second before letting go of me. They vamoosed.

I straightened out my shirt, looked him in the eyes and said, "Thank you."

He flinched and fidgeted. He looked over to the field and then at the ground. "My sister's gay," he whispered and jogged over to the coach before I could say a word.

The back of my eyes felt hot. Man, my stomach hurt. I couldn't believe he told me that. The way he said it felt like he had never said it out loud before. The knowledge was sacred.

I decided this time to be in the exact center of the bleachers, so everyone could see me. Hollow-sounding metal alerted everyone to my presence, and Kid waved — perfect gay guy thing to do, I must say, but don't ask me why.

I waved back and decided to watch, as opposed to pulling out some of my homework and being studious. I paid special attention to Richard, thinking about what he had told me. Despite his awkward height, he moved like he had complete control of every inch of his being. In comparison, I could be considered a klutz.

The practice was mostly boring, though the parts where Kid got to participate were funner. God, this is going to sound so gay, but he really does move like a dancer. I don't know what it is. He was doing the same thing all the other guys were doing, and yet it was different. Man, that Kid has skill.

At the end, the team walked off the field, and Kid stood next to the coach, presumably waiting on Carr's deliberation.

Finally, I saw Carr acknowledge Kid's presence. Kid nodded, and they talked for a moment. Carr lowered his clipboard and walked away.

I watched Kid so closely that my eyes dried. I saw no jump for joy — of course, Kid is not in character quite as much as I am. He walked toward me. His stature was his typical one. Shoulders curled ever so slightly inward. Head held high, but bent slightly down. Long, slow, easy steps. No discernible indication of whether he made it or not. I could not contain my curiosity and used my short little legs to propel myself forward.

"So?"

His face looked sunken.

I didn't breathe. That had to be devastating.

"I made it," he screeched at me.

First thing I did was throw an angry punch at his arm. "You bastard," I said. "You made me think you didn't get it."

He nodded with an air of cockiness. "I'm good, right?"

"I hate you... congratulations."

We started walking. He jutted his chin upward and stared at the clouds. "So, you think I'm good?"

"At football?"

He hesitated, but nodded.

"Kid, you're amazing."

"Really?"

"Yeah, god, it's like watching a battle, y'know, in slow-mo on TV. The main character is just massacring the other guys and he jumps over a fallen foe and they show the slow rippling of his shirt or something in the wind or a single leaf falls to the ground and... that's what it looks like."

He turned and looked at me. "That almost sounds beautiful."

"It is."

He didn't say anything, and I wondered if I made him uncomfortable. But is it really gay for a straight guy to say something is beautiful? Yes? Well, then, I guess we have that one solved.

"I like the captain, Richard Fletcher," I said.

Kid snapped to attention. "What?" he said. His voice came out thin.

"Richard Fletcher, the really tall guy, football captain. I think he's cool." Yeah, no, I wasn't going to tell him about Jared and his goons. Just because he's my friend doesn't mean he has to fight my battles or even get involved. I will maintain whatever masculinity I still possess, thank you very much.

"Oh, that's cool." Kid stared at the ground.

"Yep, you should kiss his ass every chance you get, because he's like the end all, be all for any decision on the team."

"Good to know. Thanks."

"Yep, I'm in the know."

Kid laughed. We were quiet until we got to my house.

I stopped at my front door and looked up at Kid. "Hey, thanks for doing this. I know it sounds really gay and all, but it makes sense in my mind."

He shook his head. "No, it's fine."

"Well, if you ever want anything, just ask." I opened the door and grabbed Kid's hand at the same time. Gay thing is, goosebumps rose on the entire right side of my body. Maybe my hormones had started to work at just that moment, and any touch was "exciting."

The door swung open, and the front room was empty, so I yelled, "Kid's here!"

My sister was down the stairs before I had time to take a full breath.

Then I watched Dad emerge from the kitchen, his large hand swallowing Mom's small one. His large mouth spread into an even larger grin when he locked eyes with me. He winked in approval of Kid.

I don't know if I was smiling or frowning, but Dad did not hesitate in the least. He went right up to Kid and shook his hand and then pulled him into his famous bear hug.

They were basically the same height, and it was funny how similar they looked side by side. Sure, Dad's hair was wholly darker than Kid's dark blonde. And Dad's eyes were brown while Kid's were this weird blue. And Kid's nose was sharper. And Dad was more thick. But, god, they looked more like father and son than Dad and me. I felt a pang of jealousy in my throat.

"Nice to meet you, sir. I'm Glen Seaberg."

"Hi, Glen. My, you're quite a catch. I'm David."

"Thank you, sir."

"Call me David."

"Yes, si – David."

Dad's face lit up like no one's face can. "So, let's go sit in the kitchen and get friendly."

"Okay."

I gave Kid a smile and pushed him in front of me. We all sat around the breakfast table. It was like a family affair.

"Your son is wonderful," Kid said awkwardly.

Dad nodded. "Yeah, who could ask for a better one!" I frowned. Mom could. Most people could.

"Have you guys done it yet?" Lily blurted out. Her eyes looked devilishly excited. Man, I think I could have turned to ash right there. My sister squealed when she saw my face. "You did it, oh my god. You did it!"

I froze up. I physically couldn't move.

"I suppose it's okay, but I trust you guys are being safe about it," Dad said sternly.

I opened my mouth, and I couldn't say a word. My stomach was trying to reject my food. I was never going to eat at this table again. How could they be talking so casually about it?! My god, at least Mom looked alarmed.

But Kid saved me. "We're fifteen and sixteen!" He was red. "We're not doing anything!" I felt his hand shaking uncomfortably in mine.

My panic lulled, and I was able to speak. "We're not doing anything, Dad." I had a brilliant idea. "We've decided to wait."

"Depends what you mean by 'anything'," Lily laughed. "Apparently at Denise's party they were like totally doing everything but."

"We were not. We only kissed. God, girls are stupid. You exaggerate way too much. It was a kiss. Just a kiss. God." *And not even a real one at that*, I added in my mind. I don't know why I didn't just tell them the truth.

Dad reached out both of his hands to grab my hand and Lily's. "Look, it doesn't even matter how far. I just don't want anyone getting hurt." He directed his last comment at Kid.

I felt my heart try to leap out through my mouth. My dad actually seemed a little territorial and over-protective. Any of that, though, was gone the next second when he switched the subject. "So, are you into sports, Glen?"

Kid, still as red as a tomato, licked his lips. "Yeah, yeah, I am. I tried out for the football team today and made the team."

"Well, congratulations!" Dad roared. Dad launched into a long memory about his football days.

Kid and Dad dominated the night, though Dad never ceased to include me and Lily and Mom.

It had been dark for a very long time when I insisted that Kid go home. I pushed him out the door and followed him out. Before I shut the door, Lily screamed, "French kiss him!"

I shut the door and started walking. When we far enough from the house, I whipped around and faced Kid. "I'm so sorry. If I had known that Lily would say that, I would have never even have dreamed of asking you to come." I waited for him to respond.

He took a step toward me. His eyes were power-ful-looking. Would he really hit me? I mean, no one outside my family would ever know that my sister accused us of having done it.

"I know you're gonna hate me, but I didn't mean to subject you to that. I'm sorry. Really, really sorry." I looked him straight in the eyes, so he'd know I was sincere.

And suddenly, it was as if a switch had gone off in his head. He looked down to the side, embarrassed. He grabbed his right arm. He opened his mouth and said, "Sorry, I forgot rule number two."

He was apologizing to me? My friendly rule? He hadn't broken it at all. I remembered the previous Friday morning he had said he had broken rule two that time too. What did he think my rule meant? I just didn't want him saying that we weren't friends.

"I'm sorry," he said, again, louder.

I didn't say anything. Was he playing some sort of joke on me? I was taking advantage in every possible way. For god's sake, we were pretending to be gay. I was even pretending to be gay to my family, lying to them. And he was apologizing to me for a rule he didn't even break? He didn't have to take my rules as seriously as he did.

"I'm sorry," he said, louder. He looked at me, then squeezed his eyes shut. "I'm sorry." Louder still. He clenched his fists.

I didn't know what to do. He was really upset, and I didn't even know why.

"I'm sor – "

And I had thrown my arms around him. I swear, my body did it of its own accord. God, what if I really were gay? I mean, everything up to this point had been a show for others, but no one was there. And I hugged him. I mean, it wasn't one of those brotherly love hugs. You know the ones, one arm over the shoulder in a very manly way — and the bodies don't touch... ever — but this was different. The side of my face was against his chest. My arms were wrapped so tight that you would have thought they were super glued to him.

I felt like crying. I don't know why. But my nose stung, and I fought against it. "Don't apologize." My voice came out squeaky and thin.

Gay, gay, gay, gay, until I felt Kid's arms hug me back. Then I thought maybe it wasn't so weird that I'd hug him. Maybe it wasn't so blatantly gay.

I let go of him. He peered down at me. His face was red, but there was a faint smile on his mouth.

I felt too embarrassed to say anything and just pushed him toward his house. Then, I ran away like a frightened little girl.

~

Wednesday, I couldn't look anyone in the eyes, especially not Kid.

~

Wednesday night, I lay in my bed, and I finally let myself really think about it. On Tuesday night, I had just cranked the volume up on my iPod and fallen asleep. But now, I stared at the black ceiling.

The blanket was cold, and I shivered to warm it up and maybe, hopefully, avoid thinking about it.

I hugged him. But he hugged me back, so maybe it wasn't so gay. But then again, how could you not hug someone back? So then, what was my initial motivation for hugging him? I don't know. I just did. What about Dad? He hugged Kid, too. But that was different. It was the kind of hug you gave your son — or possible son-in-law, for all Dad knew. Thinking that made my stomach ache. They matched. They looked like what a proper father and son ought to look like. I wasn't in that picture.

And I hugged Kid. I hugged him for real. For-real real. A real hug, a hug that felt more real and meaningful than any hug before. Could that entail more than feelings of friendship? Could it just be that he was the best friend I'd ever had and that we grew so close so fast that I couldn't stand him being upset? Did that happen? I mean, if we were girls, I don't think I would have even questioned my motives, but guys are different. We aren't allowed the same kind of friendships as girls and still be straight. Are we? I mean, who says we can't? Have guys done it? I couldn't think of one instance. Maybe girls are just more comfortable in themselves to have such a deep friendship. Maybe I'm just that comfortable with myself.

But if I was so comfortable, would I even be questioning my motives in the first place? I hugged him, and I knew it wasn't entirely chummy even though I was trying to convince myself otherwise.

I turned onto my side and looked toward my window. I couldn't see his window, but I imagined I could.

Did I find him attractive? Yes, well maybe. I mean, I *know* he's hot, just like I *know* his sister is hot. I think everyone can tell if someone is generally hot. I mean in our culture there are certain attributes that contribute to "hotness" and we all know them. So you straight guys who always ask if another guy is good-looking, don't fool yourselves. You know. But there was a difference. I knew that instinctively but didn't want to acknowledge it. Virginia was stunning, and I knew that. But I suppose the difference was that Glen's beauty hit me in the face, as opposed to my recognition of Virginia's beauty. I was fully aware of it in a way that I wasn't of Virginia. And did this difference make me gay? Was that all it took? Grandeur smacking me upside the head?

It seemed too simple and too easy. I mean, come on. It would be utterly clear to anyone that Kid was gorgeous. George Rekers himself couldn't deny it. You couldn't look at Kid and say he wasn't splendid. The straightest guy in the world would acknowledge it. A lesbian would acknowledge it.

Kid was just that beautiful. No other guy was so beautiful that I had to acknowledge it — well, no other girl either but I'm not going to go into that. It was Kid, I told myself. Kid was just one of those people who possessed what anyone had to acknowledge. That had to be it.

I decided that that was it and closed my eyes, but I hadn't really solved anything.

I opened my eyes, and it was Thursday morning, and I hadn't moved all night.

I turned onto my side. Everything ached.

I got ready for school, but I kept looking over at Kid's window.

I'd shut my eyes tight and chosen not to think about it.

I sat down at the kitchen table. Dad was there reading the paper. Mom was putting every ounce of herself into making the perfect pancake, but she didn't realize her effort was futile. Lily must have still been sleeping, though she was usually better at waking up than I was.

"Remember the family's getting together next weekend," Mom said to me in the middle of her impossible feat.

"Again?" I asked.

"It's been a year since we went to Uncle Bennett's house. Don't you miss your cousins? You and Jack always have so much fun."

No, I don't miss Jack or Emmett or Peter or Terrence or Ryan or even seven-year-old Shelby, I thought. They pick on me like you wouldn't believe, and when we were little, I would always have to be the indian while they were the cowboys. These boys were vicious. And Shelby was a crafty and evil genius whose one mission was to make me crap my pants every time she saw me. Two years back — when she was five, mind you — she devised a little plan in which I ended up crying and dripping with week-old fish guts. AND SHE DIDN'T GET IN TROUBLE! Riddle me that. I mean, she must have really put some planning into that one, because she even went to the trouble of acquiring fish guts.

Luckily, our uneven battle would be on my turf this year, so I had home field advantage. I was already concocting an overly complicated plan consisting of six water balloons filled with vinegar when Dad opened his mouth. "Why don't you invite Glen for the festivities?"

I could feel the blood just flooding my face. I couldn't invite Kid. I definitely couldn't invite him. And there were so many valid reasons. I mean, first and foremost, what if I really was gay? I mean, I had reasoned my way out of homosexuality the night before, but what if I was wrong? No, that would be too embarrassing. Then, there was Kid. I could see how much it pained him to pretend for me in front of my parents and Lily. It looked like he was going to cry on Tuesday night. And even if my first two reasons weren't good enough — and I definitely couldn't tell them to Dad — I was sure that family wouldn't just accept my gayness. Family get-togethers were hotbeds of prejudice, repudiation, and hurt. The cousins would just completely pummel me. I decided this was the only reason I could voice out loud. "Dad, I can't do that."

"Why not? There's nothing to be embarrassed about."

Oh yeah, there was, but I knew that wouldn't work. "Dad, they're gonna hurt me. I know it. They already pick on me as it is, but now, they would have a reason."

"I'll stop them. I wouldn't let them hurt you, ever."

"Yeah, you say that now, but you aren't there every second. I mean, those boys will find ways."

"I'll stop them, trust me."

"You can't stop them every time, Dad. I mean, I know. There's not always someone there. Like on Tuesday, I was at school, and these guys on the football team were gonna hit me. Luckily, someone stopped them, but it was luck – "

Dad was suddenly and visibly angry. "You're getting picked on at school?"

"Dad, it was only once, and someone stopped them – "

He stood up. "This is ridiculous."

"Dad."

"I'm going to have a talk with your administrators. This is absolutely unacceptable. School is supposed to be safe. You shouldn't have to worry about bullies."

"Dad, don't do anything." I grabbed him and yanked him to sit.

He calmed down and looked at me. "It's unacceptable. But you should never feel scared, and I insist that you invite Glen now. I'll fix everything."

And that was the end of that. I couldn't say anything more. He was going to take care of it. That meant there was nothing I could do to stop him.

I ate my pancake and went to school. At lunch, I ate my Chinese takeout from the skinny lady with Kid. I stared out of the school toward the parking lot, and I saw Dad marching towards the administration office. I chewed and let him be on his way.

"So, you want to hang out after school today?" Kid asked me.

It was the first time he'd asked to hang out instead of vice versa. I smiled. "Sure, man."

"At my house?"

"Sure… yeah, then I get to see the inside."

"Could you wait for me? I actually have football practice that lasts for an hour longer than school."

I shrugged. "I don't mind."

Two and a half hours later, Kid raced out onto the field like an eager beaver — see, I told you I was cliché, even in my descriptions — while I made my way toward the bleachers — I made sure that Jared and his goons weren't within fifty feet of me. He was the first one onto the astroturf. I chuckled silently.

"I told her she was disgusting and that she should die."

The voice was sad and embarrassed. I stopped and turned to face its owner. Richard looked away from me.

"My sister and I used to be really close."

"And now?"

"She went to college on the East Coast."

"Well, don't you talk to her on the phone?"

"She hasn't called."

"Have you apologized?"

Richard looked at me and shook his head. "I can't do that."

"Why not?"

He shook his head again and ran over to the field.

I found my place on the bleachers and sighed. Richard, poor kid, but come on, swallow your pride. She can't be the one to reach out after you said that to her; you have to. Even I know that, even if I know nothing.

Kid ran circles around those guys. Man, why was he even bothering with high school? He should have just gone pro already.

He was the last one off the field.

"Dude, you're so slow," I said, laughing.

"Oh, sorry. I just like being there."

We walked to his house, but Kid kept looking at me funny. Please, I wished, don't let him think I'm really gay. Finally, he said something I wasn't expecting. "What did you and Richard talk about?"

I grinned at him. "I'm not telling." What Richard said to me was in confidence.

"Oh." His head drooped. "Okay."

Had to love this Kid. The smallest, most insignificant thing got his panties in a twist.

I liked his house. It had this indie feel to it, especially with the numerous boxes stacked everywhere. His parents weren't home, but I said hi to his little sister, Allison.

Oh, she was adorable. The cutest thing I ever saw. Huge gray eyes. Thin blond hair in messy pigtails. A tomboyish pair of shorts and an overly frilly baby doll tank top.

Virginia glared at me but didn't say anything. Was she supposed to be mad at me?

I gave her my best *I-don't-care* look and followed Kid upstairs.

His room was spotless. Immaculate. "Dude, you didn't tell me you were OCD," I said, chuckling.

Kid's mouth hardened. "I'm not OCD."

"Dude, just a joke." I launched myself onto his bed, closed my eyes for a second. "I could get used to this. Wanna come over and clean my room?"

He shrugged. "If you want me to."

I wasn't sure whether to laugh or scream. This Kid was so easygoing and willing to be ordered around that I bet I could get him to do anything. "Suck my dick."

His head drew back. "What?"

I grinned. "Just checking to see if you'd do anything I suggested. Man, you're a pushover. Don't always just shrug and say sure or whatever all the time."

He clenched his teeth.

Even when he was angry, I mused. Even when he was angry, he was undeniably beautiful. "So... you like anyone? Besides my sister?" I asked.

There was a pause before he answered. "Obviously."

"Who is it?"

"You know."

"No, tell me."

"No."

I put on my best girly-pouty face. "Aww, tell me. It makes me sad when you don't tell me."

"I would be breaking rule number two. You're just trying to mess with me. Or making me lie, and I won't do that." Kid leaned against the wall and folded his arms over his chest.

I frowned. "What's this rule number two crap? I just meant that I didn't want you pulling that friendly crap on me."

"And I'm not."

"Telling me who you like wouldn't be pulling the friendly crap on me."

"Yes, it would."

I held up my hands. "Fine, fine. Don't tell me. You're so weird."

He sighed and said he was going to get a coke.

I waited and stared at the ceiling. I didn't understand Kid at all. Sometimes he was so defensive and weird and particular about the smallest thing. What in the world went on in his head?

He came back in.

"Sorry," I said. "I'm just a bit pushy, I suppose." I stretched my arm up and grabbed his shirt. "I won't ask again." He nodded. "Now, come and make hot make-up sex with me." I grinned and laughed. I had used my most nonchalant voice, but my stomach squeezed.

At first he was red, but he chuckled.

"Ah, see? Sex solves everything."

"I thought that was money."

"No, it's sex. Trust me."

~

Sunday, I asked Kid to be my gay lover. For the family reunion, only for the family reunion. God, you people jump to conclusions.

"Hey, Kid. Want to be my gay lover again?" Yes, I actually said that. No, I have no shame. All for comedy, I swear. No ulterior motives whatsoever. I swear.

He flinched but didn't take his eyes off *Call of Duty 4*. "For what?"

"My dad insists that you come to our annual family reunion."

"Oh. When?"

"Well, the family is coming on Friday and they stay until after Christmas. I would think one day would be enough."

"Sure, I'll do it."

"Thanks. You're the best gay lover ever."

He peeled his eyes off the screen and looked at me.

"Yep, our kisses are magical."

His face cracked and a grin appeared.

"You're gorgeous. A real hottie."

"You're cute too."

I covered my mouth and fluttered my eyelashes. "Oh, you're too much. And you're an *animal* in the sack."

He laughed, but he was a slight shade of pink.

"Uncomfortable yet?" I asked.

He shook his head.

What I did next was not gay. Not gay at all. I wrapped my legs around his torso. Okay, so maybe it is a little gay, but that isn't necessarily a reflection on me, is it? A cool straight guy would do it, too, in my situation. Of course, I don't know how a guy would get himself in such a weird situation. "What about now?"

He was redder, but he shook his head.

I snaked my arms around his chest and laid my head on his shoulder. "Now for sure."

He laughed and shook his head. "I can't be conquered."

Then, I did something even more gay. I kissed him on the cheek. I don't know if I could say a straight guy would do that, but come on, the situation totally called for it. I had to make him eat his words. Oh, god, I must be gay. The back of my neck hurt with recognition, but I didn't let go of Kid. Because if I backed down, Kid would know that I was rattled by the fact that I kissed him. If I was gay, he absolutely couldn't know. I don't know why, but he just couldn't. I mean, then we couldn't act so comfortably around each other anymore. Though, I guess that would make more sense. Guys probably weren't supposed to make these kinds of jokes and still just be straight.

He was redder than I thought he could be and just sat there.

I grinned. "Ha, I'm good. I broke you."

He gave me a thin but defiant grin. "No, you didn't."

Man, this guy was the straightest straight guy ever. I mean, he still had the guts to say I didn't get him. He must be strong, because he had to know what was coming after this. Any normal straight guy would lose his cojones at this point.

I shook my head. "Dude, I won't back down. If you don't admit defeat, I'll have to keep going. And I can't be held responsible for my actions."

He just raised his eyebrows, challenging me.

"Dude, you're asking for it." And I grabbed his face, which shot chills down my spine. Gay, gay, gay, gay, gay, gay, kiss, gay, gay, gay, gay, gay, oh my god gay.

My first kiss. Was it supposed to feel so strong? I mean, I could feel it down to my toes. I could feel it pulling at my crotch. My head buzzed. My throat got this hollow feeling.

And... did he kiss me back?

I looked at him.

He stared back and then averted his eyes. He did, didn't he?

As if on some unspoken signal, we pulled back from each other. He slid onto the floor, and I crawled to the farthest corner of my bed.

Call of Duty 4 was the only noise in the room.

"Sorry," he said.

"No, I'm sorry," I said.

We didn't say anything until he left.

I didn't know what to think. Everything failed me. I felt terrible, but I was smiling. No doubt that was gay. I liked kissing him, no doubt about that. So, then, did that make me definitively gay? No doubt about that either? Well, if being gay was feeling like that, then I don't think I mind.

We avoided each other at school the next day and the next day, which was the first finals day. It felt weird not talking to him, making inappropriate jokes about sex and women and Mr. Werely and his pedophile status. It was like before he moved here, and I was amazed at how short and long it had felt.

Virginia came up to me looking completely exasperated. She threw her hands up. "Warren, you better tell me, because Glen's refusing. What happened? Why are you guys being so weird?"

I stared at her and then looked away. "Um, if Kid doesn't want to tell you, I don't think I should tell you."

She sent her death rays at me. "Fine."

She left me, and I sat down at the nearest table to eat my bagel. My second period final was next, and I was worried about it. Except I was thinking more about other things.

I took my final and went home. Who doesn't love minimum days?

I didn't study for my next two finals that afternoon. I looked up gay porn on the internet. Haha, no, no, I swear, I didn't. I'm fifteen, sheesh. Don't take me so seriously, though maybe it's more realistic that I would look at porn, I don't know anymore. But I was on the internet, because the internet holds infinite wisdom, and I am Socrates, the humble unearther of wisdom. Want to know what I typed into Google?

Yep, I am one hundred percent original. I typed in "am i gay." It felt weird even writing out those words into a search engine.

Most of the results were dumb "Are You Gay?" quizzes that relied on me knowing if I was gay already. One result was a boy's tale about how he had "struggled with homosexuality." He also said that he was jealous when his guy friends got girlfriends. I thought about that, but it didn't help me, because Kid was my first and only friend in years, and as far as I knew, he didn't have a girlfriend.

I looked at other results. Some said that I might be if I had same-sex feelings. That didn't help me either, because Kid was a god. I kissed him, but girls kiss each other and they are still completely straight. So wouldn't that apply to guys kissing too?

I closed the browser and felt like vomiting. I was sure that kissing didn't necessarily mean attraction, right? Girls could do it without any emotional attachment whatsoever. I mean, it's like a party favor to them — some, okay, not all, just some. The fact that we kissed didn't mean anything.

Maybe, since I have no experience whatsoever, I would have gotten overexcited with just any kiss. I closed my laptop and pushed it away from me. I lay down and stared at the ceiling.

What did gay mean, anyway? It certainly couldn't be something physical, because then gay people who had sex with the opposite sex would be straight and gay at the same time. So, a state of mind? A miniscule chemical reaction? A minor DNA variation? God, it was maddening. What was the point at which you were gay? How far did your mind go before it was obviously gay?

No definitive answer to that question, according to the internet. You just had to "decide that out for yourself." I hate gray areas. Then, I could just say, "I'm straight," and leave it at that?

Okay, I'm straight; I just like to pretend I'm gay, for laughs — only for laughs, not because of some inner desire to let my "same-sex feelings" out. Wow, that's believable.

~

Friday came, and I at least passed my finals.

Mom was dusting the mantel when the doorbell rang. She bustled over and called for Lily and Dad to come downstairs and greet the family. I stood at attention in my usual spot for the hugs and the hellos and the hell deliverance.

Uncle Bennett burst through the door before Mom had gotten it open an inch. His burly arms enveloped Mom, and she squeaked. "Cecily, you look more gorgeous every time I see you! Why did David get the prettiest woman?" Uncle Bennett was unhappily divorced — or happily if you want to put it that way. Aunt Veronica had been... difficult, to say the least.

His three sons followed. Peter, the oldest cousin, took his place first in line sporting his senior football jacket. Jack, my age and second oldest cousin, rested against the door jamb waiting for everyone to move out of his way. Ryan, the seventh-grade swim star, hung on Jack's shoulder, trying to look inside.

Dad roared with laughter from the staircase. "No trading!" They did their manly brother hug thing, and Uncle Bennett caught sight of me.

His face changed instantly. It wasn't one of disgust or anything. It was just so downer-y. Like I had spoiled the mood. Obviously, Dad had told them.

He did something so unfamilial that it was like he had spit in my face. He jammed his hand under my nose and waited for me to shake.

I looked up at him and grinned. If they were going to treat me like rotten fish, I might as well act however I can to get them upset. I spread my arms and stuck to him like glue. "Oh, Uncle Bennett. You should see him. He's gorgeous. And he kisses like a proper demon. So sexy. I can't wait for you to meet him. You guys'll love each other!" My heart skipped when I said "kisses," but I kept my face completely in character.

Uncle Bennett was red. A proper red. The red that you imagine when someone says "red-faced," not the typical pink.

Dad's hand rested on my shoulder. He nodded at Bennett. "You will love Glen. He's a good kid."

I nodded eagerly and let go of my uncle. I had enough fun with him for the moment. I turned to my oldest cousin and winked. "Hey, Peter! Miss me?"

He was better equipped to deal with my performance. He shrugged. "Yeah, sure."

I pulled him into a hug and decided to take it further. I whispered in his ear, "He's so big. Makes me hurt, but feels so good." I knew it was outrageous to say — not to mention highly inappropriate and probably not something a gay guy would say to make his family accept him, but hey, all for comedy and spite — but his reaction was worth it. He stiffened and straightened up. His face was white.

All in a good day's work.

I moved on to Jack, my true nemesis and tormen-tor. What would make him uncomfortable to the greatest extent? Lightbulb! I hugged him and whispered, "Hey, y'know, if you're into it, my friend Seth said he really likes guys who're into soccer, and uh, you're just his type."

He pushed me back, not caring that the adults were right there.

I shrugged at him and just grabbed Ryan. My overly feminine hug was enough to, pardon the pun, scare him straight.

I turned sharply and marched to the kitchen to help Mom with whatever she needed. I couldn't help myself and snickered while getting Mom's pre-prepared fruit platter.

I swooped over to the couches where my cousins and Lily were seated. "Fruit? Anyone?" I set it down on the coffee table and plopped down in the only empty seat, between Jack and Peter.

I crossed my legs, because that seems very gay.

"Hey, Warren. I was just telling them how hot, with a double t, Glen is. What day did you say he was coming?" Lily asked me. She was having as much fun as I was, but for different reasons.

I shrugged. "He didn't say." I didn't know if he was still going to come. It was vital for my revenge on my cousins that he came, even if was totally awkward between us.

"Oh. What are you getting him for Christmas?"

My eyes widened. I had to get him something for Christmas? I didn't want to buy him anything. What would I get for him? Socks? It had to be something gay, but I wracked my mind for something that wouldn't be expensive as hell — you gays sure have expensive tastes. "I'm gonna take him on the best date of his life." That was the best thing I could think of? God, that was too gay. I didn't want Kid to think I was gay, just everyone else. If I asked him on a date — even a fake one — it'd be like saying I was gay — yeah, because kissing him was not gay at all.

Lily squealed. "Oh my god, let me help plan it!"

"Uh, sure."

She clapped in a very bimbo-type way.

I rested my hand on Peter's shoulder — yeah, because I'm "gay" means I'll come onto any guy, even my cousin. "Any suggestions, Peter?"

He looked at me, frowning. He shook my hand off and shook his head.

"Jack?" I asked, gripping his arm.

He withdrew his arm and said, "No." Quietly, he whispered, "You're a fag. Don't touch me."

I ignored his second comment and whipped my head around to face Lily. "Why are these guys acting so weird?"

Lily smiled and winked at me — for once, she was on my side — because she understood I was using my perceived homosexuality as a weapon (of mass destruction). "I don't know. Is it hot in here or something?"

"Well, if Kid was here, it'd be even hotter," I said, chuckling.

Lily shrieked with laughter. "Maybe you should invite him over right now? Be nice and toasty."

I laughed but shook my head. I wasn't ready to talk to him yet, much less ask him to act like my gay lover. "Maybe tomorrow, once everyone's here."

Lily switched the subject to Peter's football, and my cousins actually started talking.

I sat there and didn't say a word, because what the hell did I know? I didn't say anything, until Lily dragged me in.

"Glen's on the football team, isn't he?"

I looked at her and nodded. "Yeah, when he's practicing, it's beautiful. I could watch him all day. And he loves it. You can see it. Makes me love watching him even more." I sucked in a sharp breath, surprised that I wasn't acting.

Lily giggled. "I wanna see. He's absolutely gorgeous, isn't he?"

"Yeah," I said, not paying her any attention. In my mind, Kid was on the field. God, thinking about him on the field made my throat ache and feel empty, like I had felt when we had kissed.

Dad chose that moment to come over, glowing from his interaction with his brother. "Hey. Why don't you guys go out into the backyard and play a little touch football?"

Before any of us knew it, we were in Dad's whirl-wind of enthusiasm for a game of football in our sardine can of a yard. Lily, of course, was able to excuse herself, like always.

Dad tossed me the football and went to rejoin Bennett in the dining room.

I smiled like my life depended on it. "So," I said. "Who wants to be on my team?"

I ended up with Ryan. The smallest of the three. And we started our game, which basically consisted of a makeshift form of wrestling. The goal was to get the ball to touch the wall opposite your team, by any means necessary.

And by "any means necessary" I mean trying to get enough "accidental" kicks and elbows to my face and gut and legs as humanly possible. I felt like I had gone through a meat grinder after three rounds.

Want to know the worst part? Ryan, who was supposed to be on my team, hit me several times "by accident" but didn't once touch his brothers. The fourth round: Peter stepped on my hand. The fifth round: Jack kneed me in the groin.

The "game" was worse than usual, but then again, I had provoked them. And since I'm a masochist, I provoked more.

Breathing raggedly through a bloody nose, I grinned at the ground. I was on my hands and knees trying to spit all the brownish-red blood infused saliva out of my mouth. I laughed. "Wow, you guys are good and very pretty, too. Nothing compared to Kid, but pretty all the same." It's like I don't even have to be that clever to get them all upset.

"Next round!" Jack barked instantaneously. And I got up, and he got a choice fist into my stomach as he plowed past me with the ball. Two more rounds. God, when was someone going to stop this? My eyes watered with the pain in my nose.

"Y'know what? I'm gonna go inside," I breathed, hoping that just this once, they would let me. Jack steered me back into my place.

Another round. Another elbow to my face. God, it hurt. It hurt like bloody hell. This was why I hated when we got together. And even if someone watched them play, they never saw the well placed attacks on me. And I was never let to go inside until Dad or Mom or Uncle Bennett or Aunt Delia or one of the adults saw my condition and ushered me inside, chirping about how I always got so hurt and that the other boys ought to be more careful. Thank god Dad hadn't sent us to the park like three years ago. They had left me there when it was past dark and said that I had run off and that they looked for me for a long time.

"I don't think this is football." The voice came from above. It was Kid's voice. I looked up. He was sitting on the wall between our yards. He must have climbed the tree in his yard to get up there, but I hadn't heard him. He gave my cousins a little wave. "I'm Kid, but call me Glen."

I could have kissed him I was so happy — and not for the gay reasons, either. And was he cool, like a proper superhero swooping in to save the damsel in distress — that's me — in the nick of time — before I was so damaged that I needed to go to the hospital, like three years ago when they claimed a mugger must have gotten me and I was too delirious to deny it.

My cousins still hadn't said anything.

"How 'bout this," he said. "Three against two. Me 'n Warren against you guys. I think that's fair." He jumped off his perch and landed in our yard. He helped me up. "Hey, man. How're you doing? Sorry, if I had known, I would have come sooner."

"Uh, thanks." I looked up at him and sniffed to keep the blood from dripping out of my nose. "Sorry about Sunday."

He shrugged. "I won."

I gave him that one. I don't think my masculinity could handle taking it any further than a closed mouth kiss. I grinned, but it hurt my face.

He smiled at my cousins. "So, what's the score? I only want to play until we beat your sorry asses."

Oh god, sweet revenge. He had me stand at the furthest wall, and, having no qualms about someone doing the dirty work for me — yeah, that gender norm of a man always defending his honor and such just never made sense to me — I just watched.

My face felt hot, and I don't think it was just from the injuries I sustained.

God, Kid was amazing. He dodged and leapt and flew past them and made the first goal. They tried to pummel him all at once, but he would just ram through them and break through to the other side. Once Jack ran toward me in order to use me as a sort of hostage, but without Jack joining his brothers in their defense,

Kid made a goal faster and yelled that this round was finished before Jack could touch me.

I loved having Kid on my team. He beat them good, and without leaving so much as a mark on them, which was so ironic and hysterical — though I kind of wish he had beat them to a bloody pulp — hey, I'm not a pacifist.

Kid pushed me inside once he had left my cousins utterly speechless. Yeah, they didn't know that my fake boyfriend was that gorgeous or that amazing at football.

Mom fretted over the state of my face as soon as she saw me. I wondered what I looked like.

But I saw myself soon enough in the reflective surface of the oven. God, my right eye was almost hidden by the puffy flesh surrounding it. My nose looked even more crooked than usual. And my complexion, below the nose, was this lovely shade of brownish-red. Dried blood does wonders for opening up the pores.

It actually looked worse than it felt, which was a blessing. I was mostly numb.

I sat at the breakfast table and waited quietly for Mom to call Dad and rush for the first aid supplies, though I have no clue how those would help my face now. I had nothing really to put a bandaid on, unless she had a face-sized one.

"What happened?" Dad asked frantically.

Kid answered for me. "Those are some bastard kids out there. Playing dirty every chance they get."

"My boys?" Uncle Bennett asked from the doorway between the kitchen and the dining room.

Kid looked at him and nodded. He then held out his hand for Bennett to shake. "I'm Glen, by the way."

"Oh," Bennett said while shaking his hand. Ha, my fake boyfriend flabbergasted them all because he was the butch type — actually he was the straight type, but they didn't know that. I'm supposedly and obviously the femme-ish type who takes it up the ass — so I actually fit their idea of the queer, but Kid didn't. Or is the correct terminology bear and queen or something else? Is butch and femme only for lesbians? I've got to look that up. Anyway, Kid is cool like that.

Mom fussed and disinfected my face and arms with something that stung like hell. I didn't show her the rest of my body.

My cousins didn't come inside during my treatment, which is more than before. They always would talk to Mom saying they were sorry and that my skin was just too thin.

Uncle Bennett continuously looked from me to Kid, like he just didn't understand it. I would have grinned like a fool if my face hadn't hurt so much.

Kid stood there, stoically and all cool. I really felt as if he was my hero. My pupils must have gotten ten to fifteen percent larger as I stared at him. The grass stains on his palms and the knees of his jeans gave him this rugged adventurer look, and I can honestly say that it was sexy. Made me want to grab him, pull the collar of his shirt down and kiss him. And hope that he would kiss me back. How's that for gay?

Of course, none of that happened. Instead, I squealed like a pig getting slaughtered when Mom poured the Bactine on my hands.

Kid looked at me and then looked at my uncle. "You should control those boys of yours. This is absolutely unacceptable."

Bennett looked shocked for a second then his eyebrows snapped together. "You're telling me to control my children? You're young enough to be one of them."

Kid shrugged but gathered his shoulders up and stood at his full height. "Yeah, I'm telling you to control your children. Regardless of who I am, those boys are rotten."

Haha, Bennett was shorter than my fake boyfriend. He just shook his head. "You have no right – "

"I have all the right in the world." Kid snapped back.

And that was the end of it. I think Uncle Bennett was intimidated by Kid. Mom finished doing her best and gave me a pack of ice to help with the swelling. Dad and Uncle Bennett went outside to talk to my cousins.

I didn't feel even a bit of sorrow for those bastards like those altruistic, compassionate main characters that always pop up in stories about bullying and oppression. I'm bitter to the bone.

And I'm selfish. Because when Mom went to put her first aid kit away, I grabbed Kid's hand and held it. And this wasn't an act, because no one was around to watch. My stomach swelled. In my mind, I made rationalizations for why it wasn't gay, but none of them were good enough to even mention. "Hey, man. Uh, thank you."

"No problem. Sorry for not coming sooner. I was at practice."

I grinned at him, despite the pain — actually the Bactine numbed it more — and did my best makeshift wink. "You're the best boyfriend ever."

He didn't smile at first, but then it crept over his face. "I am, aren't I?"

"Hey, hey, don't get a big head."

He pulled away from me and went to the counter where Mom had set out a bowl of chips and some dip. He proceeded to stuff every chip he could into his mouth.

I stared at him. He chewed quickly and quite quietly despite the nature of the chip. "About Sunday – "

"What about it?"

How quick he said it forced me to look away. "Never mind."

Mom came back and Kid helped her with dinner while I leaned back in my chair and tried to relax, but Kid's presence made me feel uneasy. I couldn't stop staring. Oh, when he reached up for something in the cabinets for my mom, my breath caught in my throat. His shirt lifted up, revealing a tiny sliver of his stomach. And god, it was so hot.

He turned and looked at me. I hid my face. "Is it hurting?"

I relaxed and looked back. "Yeah, hurts like hell."

"Man up," he said and laughed.

I clutched my chest and mock-died. "Way to stab me in the heart." … Wait, that didn't come out right.

Dinner was ready, and my cousins came inside. Lily came downstairs and stared at the carnage that was my face for a few moments before ignoring me. Ryan looked completely ashamed. "Sorry," he said. "It's just so easy to pick on you, and I get carried away." He forced himself to look at me and then sat down in the seat across from me. Jack didn't acknowledge me at all. Peter nodded.

Dad got an extra chair for Kid and we all sat down for Mom's lasagna. Kid sat to my left and ate like he hadn't eaten in months. "You are an amazing cook, Mrs. Rawley," he said after swallowing a whomping hunk of pasta and sauce and cheese.

Mom giggled. "Thank you."

And everyone started their own conversations.

Kid grinned at me. "Thanks for inviting me."

"Thanks for coming." I basically picked at my food. Everything hurt too much for me to have an appetite. "So, how did your finals go?" I asked the first thing that came into my mind.

He shrugged but didn't take his eyes off the food. "I think I did well. Except maybe on my chem final."

"That damn periodic table, huh?"

"Well, kind of. It's just so much stuff to memorize."

I snorted. "Sounds like how it is for me in every class."

He didn't look at me, but said, "If you ever wanted any help, I probably could help you."

I shook my head. "Then I would have no pride left. No, I've got to fail fantastically, unaided, at something."

He put down his fork on his plate and laughed. He looked at me. I nodded in my slow *I'm-a-cool-guy* way. He nodded quickly in his sarcastic way of saying "Oh yeah, that makes sense."

Ryan stared at us. His face was pink. His eyebrows were halfway up his forehead. "So, you don't like girls?"

I didn't know how to answer that, seeing as I wasn't sure who I liked.

Luckily, Kid is my knight in shining armor — I told you I'd be punniful. "No, we still like girls. But it's completely platonic. It's just different. We like girls like you like other guys."

"So... I mean, do you guys like to wear dresses and stuff?"

I wanted to laugh. Wasn't that transgender, not gay? Whatever, if I am sure of anything, I'm sure I don't want to crossdress, at all. My masculinity is already dangerously low as it is.

Kid grinned. "No – "

"Only in private," I said, chuckling.

Ryan's face soured.

"I especially like wearing women's underwear. I'm wearing a pair right now."

And everyone at the table had gone silent.

I knew Dad was about to say something so disgustingly sweet and accepting that I blurted out, "The real challenge is getting Kid to wear them."

I think a pin dropped three miles away.

Kid roared with laughter. He slapped my back hard, which sent a blossoming of pain all over my shoulder. When no one laughed with him — though I saw my dad cracking a grin, though I'm not sure he knew it was a joke — Kid cocked his head to the side. "Don't tell me you believe this guy? Half of what he says is lies."

I folded my arms over my chest. "Hey, it's only forty nine point nine percent lies. Don't exaggerate." I grinned at my cousins. "But yeah, I say a lot of outrageous things – "

"'Cause he's an attention whore," Lily chirped.

I shrugged to acquiesce. "That's like the pot calling the kettle black."

"So, do you wear women's underwear?" Ryan asked. I guess he wasn't as shy as I thought.

I chuckled. "No. But give me a million bucks and I'll do it."

"I'd do it for a million bucks!" Lily screeched.

Ryan grinned. "Me too." His family gave him a look. Okay, Ryan was definitely cool in my book now. I forgave him that second for elbowing me in the ribs.

Dad laughed and started talking about some inconsequential historical world affair — I mean, who wants to talk about the OPEC oil crisis — with Mom and Uncle Bennett.

"Well, Ryan. I think you do that already, don't you? Without the money," I said. "I mean, you can't wear loose swim trunks in competitions, can you?"

"Not if I wanna be fast, I can't."

"Aren't the tight swimsuits like women's underwear?" I asked. Oh, it was going to be fun teasing him.

He averted his eyes.

"It's for sports. You're mean, Warren," Kid announced.

I rolled my eyes. "Oh, come on. Why can't I insult his masculinity just a bit more? It's payback." I gave him a hopeful smile.

He shook his head. Man, Kid was a controlling fake boyfriend. For a moment, I wished that the "fake" part was gone. No doubt that was gay.

Dinner was finished, and Kid and I went out into the front yard.

"So, thanks for coming today," I said, crushing the leaves beneath my shoes.

"Don't let them do that to you next time. I mean, call me or something. We're friends."

I looked up him and frowned. I really was gay. For sure gay. Because I wanted us to be more than that. And just like that, there was no doubt in my mind. It was funny how suddenly being sure made me feel better. Ignorance isn't bliss. Knowing was so much better. My hands shook.

He went home.

I felt like crying. It was such an unmanly thing to do, but I did it anyway. It was quick and quiet, and I felt better afterwards. I stayed outside for a few minutes so no one would think I had cried.

Inside, Dad had started an epic game of team Monopoly. Dad and Mom were a team. Bennett and

Jack were a team. Peter and Ryan were a team. Lily glared at me, but patted the spot on the floor next to her. "You better not be so gay now that you've gone soft." I was the best at Monopoly. I had no mercy, and I was very lucky.

I sat down next to her and beat all their asses. It was an excellent distraction from the flashing neon sign in my mind.

And yet, at every quiet moment, my mind shouted it at me. It felt dirty. Like I was keeping a secret from them. But that didn't make sense, because they already knew. I just hadn't been serious up to this point. "I'm gay," I said, because I just had to say it. It didn't mean anything to them, and maybe that's why it was so easy to say.

Silence.

Lily jammed her finger into my arm. "Yeah, your boyfriend's gay too." She seemed to think it was so funny.

Dad threw the dice and shouted, "Doubles!"

We started to play again.

~

I shared Lily's bed that night. It was awkward. When we were little, it was fun and all, but now, no.

"You're so gay," she said.

"Yeah," I whispered. It was different now, because it wasn't a joke.

"So, where are you going to take him on your date?" Her eyes were bright.

Oh yeah, I had said I was going to take him out on a date as a present for Christmas. But that had been part of the acting. I couldn't actually take him on a date. We'd just have to leave my house like we were going on a date and then just hang out or something. "Where do you think?"

"I think it should be classic. Like dinner and a movie."

"A movie?" That means we'd actually have to go see it just in case they asked about the plot or something.

"Well, what else are you going to do?"

"I don't know."

"Then it should be a movie."

No use arguing with her. I shut my eyes and turned away from her.

I woke so early the next morning because my body ached. No one was awake, and it was still dark.

I crept into my room and grabbed some clothes and closed the door as quietly as possible so as not to wake Ryan or Jack.

In the bathroom, I stripped off my clothes. I looked at myself in the mirror. Not one bruise, even though it hurt like hell. I had nothing, no proof that they had hit me so many times — "on accident." I swore, though I don't know why the bruises were so important to me. I wasn't planning on showing them to anyone. I have rarely ever bruised in my life. I guess I have thick skin or something like that. I still had the cuts from the attacks to my face, but no bruises.

Even without the bruises, I looked like hell. Pale, sickly-looking chest. Arms that looked like you could break them with your pinkie. Everything on me was small, except maybe my dick. It wasn't big or anything, just seemed big in comparison to my body. I guess I have one measly claim to manhood, though few people will ever see it. My face was all angles and not good ones.

My hair was thick though, like Dad's. Everything else was Mom, weak and breakable.

I always felt miserable after our "games." It took a while to sink in, but that feeling of ultimate vulnerability and weakness always set.

I couldn't even fend them off. Someone always had to do that for me, and, logically, needing to be saved wasn't so bad. But it happened every damn time.

I don't have a problem with not being the strongest, but I do have a problem with being so weak and unable to defend myself. I might deny it and say I don't, but I do. Looking at the fragile body in the mirror was so upsetting because I don't feel weak. I walk around like I am just as strong and able as everyone else, but ultimately, I'm not.

I turned on the water and climbed into the tub. I sat and played in the water half-heartedly.

I stayed in the water until I felt cold. A quick shampoo, and I pushed down on the thing that made the tub drain.

Breakfast was lively. Peter and Jack were arguing about sportsy things, but I couldn't make heads or tails of it. So instead, I listened to Dad whispering fiercely on the phone in the kitchen with Grandma.

"Mom, you can't do this... I don't care what the Bible says. He's your grandson... I wouldn't care if he was a green and purple fifty-toothed slug, Mom. He's my so – ... Have you actually read the Bible in context, Mom?... Yeah, it says that, but – ... Mom, it was written two thousand years ago. Times have changed... No, you're wrong... I know... I have a better relationship with God than you do... Yes, I do. You abandoned Dad when he needed you most... Love and compassion, Mom. Above all else." There was a long silence. Grandma was the only one who could make Dad ruffle his feathers. This was probably the one time I wanted to see him unshakeable, and he wasn't. "You're wrong... No, I am not going to send him away... There's nothing wrong with him... Okay, even if it were and I'm not saying it is, those places are known to do more harm than good... No, God's will is not what you think it is... All you are trying to 'promote' is hate... No, and it's not healthy... You say that, but God loves him and me and even you. If He made him this way, He doesn't want him to be changed... No, that is taken out of context. It was about hospitality, not homosexuality... I'm sure, Mom... Just come... Why not? You'll regret it later... No, I'm sure. You're making the wrong decision... Everyone else is coming... Bennett has been here since yesterday... Yes, all three boys... Thomas and Irving are coming today... Yeah, they're bringing their kids... Of course, this isn't a disease. They can't get infected. You are ill-informed, Mom. Don't listen to your pastor anymore... That man just likes the power he has over your congregation... He isn't truly a man of God if he preaches hate... Don't say it again. My son has every right to be here... I will not. He shouldn't have to hide because of you... You wouldn't mind if Lily brought a boy, so there is no difference... No difference... Both relationships are equal under God... You're wrong, Mom... Okay, either you come and accept him or you don't come at all... I will do that... If that's the choice I have to make, then I'll never see you again... No, I won't give in... He is my son. Nothing changes that... Yeah, you're my mom, but he's my son... My children are most important to me. Whatever they want, I want... I wish you would come... Bye, then."

Lily's hand was wrapped around mine. She squeezed it and handed me a napkin.

I was surprised to find that my face was wet. Grandma, of all people. I wiped at the salty water on my cheeks. I knew she was really religious, but she always said she loved her grandchildren forever. My back hurt. It was utter rejection. Bennett and Jack and Peter, it was different with them, because they at least came, even if they thought it was wrong. They came, even if they beat me up. They came. She wouldn't even come. It was Christmas, for god's sake.

I felt a tentative hand on my shoulder. "Dude, Warren. Don't worry about Grandma. We love you. We love you, even if we can't exactly say it. Trust me, we do," Ryan said to me.

Dad strolled in from the kitchen with his head held unusually high. "Well, Grandma can't come, but she sends her love."

I stood up, went upstairs and fell face-first onto my unmade bed. It smelled like Jack's overly-powerful cologne, but I didn't care.

God damn it.

God damn it. God damn it all. God damn it all to hell.

It hurt so much. Who knew it would hurt so much? It wasn't like what happened with Peter and Jack at all. It wasn't even completely serious when they did what they did. And they'd always done that anyway. And they could at least stand being around me, but she wouldn't even come.

I turned over onto my back. "Shit." And I rubbed at my eyes. "Fuck."

I stood up and went back downstairs. They all stared at me. I sat down at my space and picked up my fork.

The eggs looked like rubber. "Fuck. FFuck. FFUCK."

Mom didn't say anything about the swearing like she usually would. "Fuck her, Warren. She doesn't matter."

I swallowed the spit gathering in my mouth and stared at her. It wasn't her nature.

She stared right back at me. I saw her fingers trembling around her knife. "She's a damned bitch if she won't come." Everyone stared at her. She didn't lose her nerve though. Her shoulders shook, but she didn't let her eyes fall.

"Yeah," I said.

"It isn't right," Dad said quietly.

I stuffed a huge forkful of eggs into my mouth.

Uncle Irving, Aunt Delia — his wife — and Cousin Emmett came at noon.

Emmett was through our front door as always, shouting something he'd never shouted. "Where's my gay?" He had me in a violent headlock before I had time to turn and run. I fought against him, but it seemed like I was trying to move a boulder. "So, Warren, I assume you're on bottom."

Everyone was just ignoring our little exchange, because Uncle Irving stepped in, laughing like a maniac and swallowing everyone in his overbearing grizzly hug.

"Let go of me," I said and tried to trip him up with my legs.

"Yeah, you're a bottom," he confirmed and nodded happily. "I always knew you'd be gay." Then he shrugged. "Or a knife-wielding maniac who'd kill us all in our sleep for revenge. Either way, but I was betting on gay."

"How do you know I'm not the knife-wielding maniac still? I've got a nice set under my bed. I sharpen them every night. Biding my time," I half-snarled, half-pleaded, half-joked.

He grinned at me, which was hard to do considering he had me in a headlock. "You're gay. You can't be both. And man, you're so gay. I can tell, even if you hadn't told everyone."

Did I really look gay? I didn't want to look really gay. I thought I just looked scrawny. How does one look gay? I stopped struggling and sighed. He would keep going. So, instead, I switched to something benign and boring. "How's New York?"

He shrugged, still not letting me go. "It's okay, I guess. I've recently gotten into sidewalk art. The door-man even lets me do it in front of our building. People take pictures of it; it's cool."

"That's cool." Damn kid wouldn't let me go.

"Oh!" He let me go and snapped his fingers. "What does your boyfriend look like?"

I didn't answer.

"Okay, is he good-looking? Because if he is, I'll draw something of you guys. But if he's ugly, I'd prefer not to, just you then." He nodded slowly. "I'm going to draw everyone before Christmas...so? Is he ugly?"

I glared at him.

He sighed. "And don't give me that crappy, 'He's beautiful to me.' I hate that. You know what's good-looking and what's not."

I dug my fingernails into my palms. "He's gorgeous. The most beautiful guy you'll ever see."

He patted my shoulder. "Good to hear. Got to get a picture of you guys together later."

Then I was in Uncle Irving's thick arms. He almost slapped my lungs out of my chest. "How're you doing, kiddo?"

"Good, Uncle Irving."

"Good to hear. Good to hear. Your boyfriend is coming, right? David told me all about you guys. I think it's wonderful that you're not afraid. Grown men

— grown, mind you — refuse to admit it and to me of all people. I wouldn't tell a soul if they didn't want me to. I once saw one of my coworkers with his boyfriend on the street. They kissed before they realized I was standing there, and when I said 'hi,' he insisted that the man was his brother. The other guy was Asian for god's sake. And just because I look like I'm some redneck wrestler in a business suit, they think I'm going to kill 'em or something. I say they shouldn't judge if they don't want to be judged." His face was red. "Me," he said. "Me! I'm like a big teddy bear. And people don't tell me anything. I mean, the other day, this lady Cheryl at the office threw a makeshift baby shower in the lounge, and I wasn't invited. My god, they must think I'm going to eat any little babies I find lying around. Yeah, and she wasn't going to tell me she was pregnant, either. Oh, and Joe! He got married! I wasn't informed until I overheard Leeanne talking about it to Nadia, because everyone in the office was invited but me. It's just ridic – "

Aunt Delia's thin long arms snaked around his huge shoulders. "Dear, dear, calm down," she said in a smooth voice. She was taller than my uncle, which is a feat in and of itself. She had some stunning travel dress on over her non-existent frame. To explain, she works for some famous designer, and it seems like everyone from the New York fashion industry is anorexic. But actually, Aunt Delia is just naturally that thin. She even likes to eat. She smiled at me. "Don't let him talk your ears off, honey." She pecked my uncle on the cheek and wrapped her arms around me. "Nice to see you. Introduce me to your boyfriend later."

Both she and Irving left me to chat it up with the rest of them.

Uncle Thomas, Aunt Carrie, Terrence and Shelby came at three. They were of the quieter variety of Rawleys, except Shelby who squeaked with laughter when she saw me. Terrence, another abnormally tall person in our family, shook my hand like he always did and nodded. After greeting everyone in the same way — except Dad and Irving who refused to accept anything less than their usual — he went to the kitchen table, where he got out his cell phone and didn't stop texting his girlfriend. Uncle Thomas hugged me awkwardly and tried to smile. Aunt Carrie grinned and hugged me. She was a small woman, thank god — coincidentally, her husband, my uncle, was the shortest of the brothers, only by three inches. We were the same height, and it was so nice.

"How're you?" I asked.

"I'm good. But that woman," she said. "That woman, Sara. Ugh, she wants partial custody of Terrence. She wasn't there when he was growing up; she gave up the right to custody when she never sent him a birthday present... ever. I'm basically his mother, in everything but blood. That woman thinks she can take Terrence back, but Tom and I won't let her. We'll win in court, for sure. But she won't stop calling in the middle of the night."

I remember Aunt Sara — or Ex-Aunt. She had always been nice, but when Terrence was six — I was five

— she just suddenly got a divorce and left, like that. Carrie married Uncle Thomas a year later and we just never spoke about Aunt Sara again. I wondered why she had suddenly made contact. "Can't you guys get a restraining order or something?"

"We're trying to do that too, but things take time," Carrie said. She looked in the direction of the kitchen. "Too much time. He just talks to that girlfriend of his all the time. I mean, she's a nice girl and all. She's head cheerleader and she volunteers. But he won't talk to me. Don't get me wrong, I'm glad he's talking to someone, but I want him to talk to me."

I nodded. Aunt Carrie talks a lot.

Mom's parents came at four; they lived just an hour away.

Mom apparently hadn't told them anything, because when Shelby screamed at me that she wanted to meet my boyfriend, they stiffened just slightly. No, they didn't say anything. They didn't say much of anything most of the time. Grandpa Vin stared at me. Grandma Rita widened her eyes at me. I nodded once at her. She nodded once in return.

And that was that. It was simple. They weren't that religious, and they had their quiet sort of love. It was just so different from my uncles and Dad. But everyone always knew that they loved us all, even Dad's side of the family. I could tell, because when I got presents from them, it was wrapped so carefully. Tape: perfectly square and equal. Folds: pressed down extra hard. Cards: painstakingly-neat lettering and a perfect heart after every "Love, Grandma and Grandpa."

The few times a year that I went to their house for the weekend they would sit and eat with Lily and me. The cutlery clinking against their plates would be the only sound until Lily launched into an overly-long story about her run-in with a rival cheerleader from another school. Grandma Rita would let a small smile grace her wrinkly face before she passed the bread basket to Lily. Grandpa Vin would slice at his meat with more vigor while listening to her story. It was that simple. Everything was so simple with them. Quiet and simple. And being at their house, it was like time stopped. I would just sit there in silence. Once in a while, one of them would say something, and it would always be so quiet and soft.

Lily was suddenly there, draping her arm on my shoulder. "You'll like him, Grandma. You too, Grandpa. Is he coming today?"

"I don't know."

"Find out." She left to talk to Carrie.

I gave Mom's parents a tentative smile and excused myself.

Emmett, Jack, Peter and Ryan were playing football in the backyard. Without me, it looked like a fair and proper game. I stood at the doorway and watched.

Emmett saw me and laughed. "You wanna join our orgy?" He punched his palm. "I can make sure you get a few real good bruises. Battles scars for all the chi – dudes!"

I shook my head.

Ryan tugged on Emmett's sleeve and said something to him.

Emmett smiled at Ryan, then at me. "I see, already bruised from yesterday, huh? It won't be as fun if I can't murder you a few times too... tomorrow, my little gay. Tomorrow, we'll have some fun."

I heard Mom call me from inside. I turned and ran inside.

Kid stood awkwardly at the front door.

My face emanated heat. I looked at him and then away at the floor.

"Hi." He scratched his arm. "I just wanted to make sure you were better today. They haven't made you play, have they?"

I shook my hea –

I was almost knocked down. Two small hands grabbed at my neck. A monkey? No, no, not a monkey, but close.

"Is this him?" she shrieked. "Is this your boyfriend?"

Kid grinned.

"What's so funny? This little monster has me in her evil grasp! Help me." I half-heartedly tried to peeled her off. Thing is, I can't hurt her, no matter how much she hurts me; she's the only one smaller than me.

"So," Shelby said in her high-pitched squeak. "Are you?"

"Yeah," Kid said slowly.

"Did he blackmail you?" Shelby asked. "How'd he get someone so pretty when he's so ugly?"

Kid snickered.

"Don't you dare laugh," I said.

He laughed. "Yes, he's got all sort of dirt on me."

"Do you have any dirt on him?"

"No."

"You're no fun."

"Yeah."

"Woah, he is gorgeous, Warren." Emmett's voice boomed from behind me. He slapped my back. "Nice catch."

"Thanks."

"So," Emmett said as he looked Kid up and down. "What's your name? You're on top, aren't you?" Shelby jumped off me, satisfied, and ran upstairs.

Kid blushed. "Glen."

"And?"

"What?"

"Are you on top?"

"Why would you need to know that?"

Emmett grinned. "I like to know. Plus, I don't see Warren being on top." What's it with Emmett's obsession with knowing who's on top?

Kid narrowed his eyebrows. His mouth hardened.

"You haven't done it yet?" Emmett said.

Kid shook his head. "We're old-fashioned like that."

"I love it! Gay virgins. That's so cute. But last I heard, Prop 8 passed. That means no marriage, right?" Emmett chuckled. He turned around and ruffled my hair. "You're gonna be bottom. Trust me." He gave Kid a little wave. "See you later, gorgeous." He laughed and went back to the game.

"Is he gay?" Kid asked me.

"No, I'm pretty sure he's straight. He's from New York."

"Oh." And that explained everything, apparently.

"Are you going to stay past dinner today?"

"You want me to?"

I looked in the direction of the dining room where all the adults were. "Yeah." I grabbed his hand. It was the first time that I really took in how it felt. It felt nice. "Everyone wants to meet you." I pulled him into the dining room. Dad saw us and smiled at me. "Hey, guys," I said.

Eight pairs — Mom was in the kitchen — of eyes on me, then on Kid. Bennett looked away. Grandma Rita and Grandpa Vin stared directly at us and waited. Irving grinned. Delia winked and smiled slowly, showing her perfectly straight and white teeth. Thomas looked straight at me. Carrie ducked her head down and rose her shoulders; she gave me a small little thumbs-up. Dad nodded slowly.

"This is K – Glen, my... boyfriend."

Kid stepped forward and bobbed his head. "Hi, guys. It's nice to meet you."

"My boss would love to get his hands on you," Delia commented.

"Excuse me?"

"My boss is a fashion designer. And he's gay. You'd be a gold mine for him."

Kid didn't say anything.

"Don't worry, honey. He's neither here nor a pedophile." Delia chuckled. "Though you don't look much like a child."

Mom came in with a basket of piping bread rolls. "Dinner will be ready soon. Can you get Shelby and Lily, Warren?" she asked me before popping back into the kitchen.

"Sit down," I said to Kid, giving him Grandma Wendy's chair and bounded out of the room.

Oh... my... god. Lily looked like a clown. I fought down my first response to laugh.

She glared at me. "Don't."

"I like the new look," I said.

"You do?" Shelby asked.

I kept my face as straight as I could and nodded.

"You'll let me do your make-up too, right? The gay guys like being girls, right?"

I shook my head.

"Oh, yes, gay guys love make-up. Warren especially," Lily said quickly.

"Okay, Warren. C'mere," Shelby said biting her lower lip and grabbing some glittery blue thing.

"Not now," I said, glad I had a reason to avoid the torture. "We're having dinner."

We all squeezed around the dinner table. Uncle Thomas, being a religious man, started to say a prayer when the doorbell rang.

"Just one moment," Mom said, putting her napkin on the table.

She came back with her sister, Michelle. Aunt Michelle looked like me, and I looked like her. So frail, so small. She shook always, like she was dying of cold. A soft wind would be the death of her, if not for the cold, because she'd fall and break her skull and let the liquid in her brain run away. Michelle smiled weakly at everyone. "Hello, everyone." Her voice came out deep, something you wouldn't expect from that mouse of a body. "Sorry, something kept me at the office." She sat down and gestured for us to continue.

Thomas began his prayer again.

"Where's Wendy?" Michelle asked when Thomas was finished.

She was met with silence; everyone had been informed about Grandma's decision regarding coming.

"She's really religious," I said, trying my best not to grit my teeth.

"And? We just prayed. I don't understand."

"I'm gay. She refuses to come, because of me. And Glen, this is Glen."

Michelle nodded slowly. "Nice to meet you," she said absently. "Never took her to be that sort. She seemed perfectly normal." She shrugged. "Well, whatever." She looked around the table. "Eat, people, eat."

Within moments, everyone had started their own little conversations. Aunt Michelle nibbled at her food. Her hands would shake a little when she didn't move them.

I noticed Uncle Bennett was saying something to me. " – says you're very good at history, and I was wondering if..." He kept saying it, but I was suddenly aware of Kid's presence. His hand was wrapped tightly around mine. His hand felt warm.

I looked at him. He looked at me. He seemed to be asking me something, but I didn't understand what he was trying to convey.

I turned back to Uncle Bennett and spouted off some nonsense answer to his question. He seemed to ponder it for a moment and then nodded.

And Kid had let go of my hand. It made me feel heavy. I liked him, didn't I?

Dinner was done. Michelle announced that she wanted to play a little poker. Betting pennies, nickels, and dimes, of course. Delia and Irving wanted to play. Dad and Emmett, too, and Jack and Peter and Carrie and Ryan. Kid sat at the table with me.

His shoulder was touching mine, because we were both leaning forward, elbows on the table. "You should play," he said. He grabbed my hand again. This time everyone saw.

My breath caught. He was so good at playing gay that it made me believe we were together, made me like it.

I decided to play — not because of any suggestion, I swear. I must be really good at bluffing, because in the end, it was just me and Michelle. Dad had run out of coins first — figures that he can't lie well. Emmett was in the final three.

Michelle stared at me with an intensity that only she can exude. "You're going down."

I shrugged. "Sure, why not." My face stretched into the widest grin possible. "But you first." Kid laughed quietly.

I won.

Michelle shook my hand good-naturedly. "I'll get you next time."

Emmett laughed. "Why is it that the runt runs circles around everyone? And why doesn't Glen play next time?"

Kid shook his head smiling. "I can't do that. I'd win too much."

~

Sunday, Kid didn't come over, and I had to sleep on the couch since my family had taken all the rooms.

After lunch, Lily steered me over to Emmett and sat down next to me. "Emmett," Lily said, putting her hands flat on the kitchen table. "Warren needs your help."

I didn't know what she was talking about.

Emmett unfolded his arms from his chest and did a sideways nod.

"He's taking Glen on a date. The best date."

"And you want help planning it?"

"Precisely."

"What have they done on past dates?"

Lily shrugged and looked at me. Finally, I was being consulted.

I felt the heat accumulating in my face. "There haven't been any formal dates," I said, feeling silly as I said it.

Emmett grinned. "A laissez-faire couple, huh?"

"Excuse me?"

"A laissez-faire couple. A phrase of my creation. Means a couple that just are together without any formality. That's cute."

"So, what should he do?" Lily asked.

"Without any previous dates, I'd say you should do something either completely typical, or be totally out-there."

I looked at him. "Real helpful, man."

He nodded slowly, showing me his teeth. "Movies, definitely then. You're not ready for a crazy date." He bit his lower lip. "It's going to be so adorable. Gay dates are too cute, especially with a guy like Glen. Man, I'd turn for that guy."

"Are you trying to tell me something?" I asked.

"No, nothing. Nothing at all. I'm just not averse to experimenting." He patted me on the back. He laughed. "I love that you're gay. Makes this family more exciting."

"I love to entertain."

"I'm sure you do. Maybe you should strip for him."

I didn't even dignify that with a response.

"You should give yourself to him in a dirty bathroom, like the old closeted gays used to do. Or give him a blow job during the movie."

I tried to smile and laugh it off, but he just had no boundaries.

"You are the cutest gay ever," Emmett told me. "You're so innocent. You should definitely take him to a movie and dinner."

"Thanks."

Lily giggled like a little school girl.

"You two are evil, pure evil," I said.

Lily handed me the phone. "Call him now. Make plans right now. I wanna scream in anticipation."

The phone was heavy. I couldn't call him without telling him beforehand. He'd think something was weird. But I couldn't not call, either. Hopefully he'd get it.

I dialed his house and listened to it ring. No answer. I smiled and told Lily. She just grabbed the phone and dialed Kid's cell phone number and handed it back to me.

It rang, and I heard Kid on the other end. "Hello? Warren?"

"Hey, Kid."

"Hi."

I breathed in and mentally crossed my fingers. "So, um, are you busy Tuesday? I was wondering if I could... take you out as a present for Christmas."

He didn't respond, but I heard him breathing. "Sure." I could imagine him shrugging. Yay, he knew what I was talking about.

"Great. I'll be at your house at six."

"Okay."

"See you later, then."

"Okay."

I pressed the "End" button and breathed out. It felt good that Kid understood me.

"So?" Lily asked.

"He said yeah."

Lily giggled. "Yay!"

"Dude, you looked scared, like he'd say no," Emmett said suddenly.

He had pinned me, but I smiled. "Yeah, I was scared, because I didn't want to wait until after Christmas break, because he leaves for football training camp on the twenty-sixth."

"An eager beaver, huh?"

"Yeah," I said. "I don't want to wait... I haven't kissed him for a while."

"He was here yesterday."

"Yeah, but you guys were here then. I can't kiss him when other people are watching."

"Denise says you were all over him during her party," Lily interjected.

"Denise exaggerates. And plus, I didn't know anyone was watching."

"Not a fan of the PDA, huh?" Emmett asked.

"No, I'm still not comfortable with all of it."

He grinned. "You will be. You'll be all over each other soon."

On Monday, Aunt Michelle made her second appearance. She had a huge bottle of wine, and she howled with laughter at the slightest joke. It's surprising that the rest of her family is so quiet.

Mom organized a huge popcorn line assembly where we strung popcorn onto fishing wire. Ryan sat next to me, and I handed him piece after piece of popcorn. Lily would shake her legs and nod vigorously every time she caught my eye.

I told Dad that I was planning on spending time with Kid tomorrow and I wouldn't be at dinner. He grinned and hugged me.

Tuesday morning, I woke up with a huge stomach ache. It didn't feel like I needed to throw up. It was apprehension about Kid's and my fake date. I texted Kid. *Hey. So, I just want to make sure you're ready for our fake date tonight. Thanks for getting what I was saying when I called you the other day. My sister and cousin were there, and I couldn't warn you. We have to see the movie, because they might ask what it was about. Don't worry. Everything is on me.*

He responded about ten minutes later with: *okay.*

Thirty minutes after that, after breakfast, I got a text message from Virginia. *BASTARD! Stop yanking Glen's chain.* I didn't understand what she was talking about, so I didn't respond.

Emmett head-locked me in the backyard. I kicked at the back of his knee, but nothing happened. "You're so weak, it's cute."

"You're ugly," I said through gritted teeth.

"No, I'm smoking hot. All the girls say so. Even a few so-inclined guys say it."

I writhed and wiggled my way out of his grip and sprinted inside.

Lily ran into me and yanked me upstairs. "You've got to pick your outfit."

"My outfit?"

"Yeah, you can't go looking like your usual slobby self."

"Why not?"

"Because this is a date. You always look your best on a date. You're clueless."

I snorted. She was the one out of the loop and clueless. Fake date, duh.

Five forty-five and I was wearing my best pair of jeans, because "I couldn't wear something more dressed up unless I was taking him somewhere where nice." They were well-fitted, very gay, but not tight. I wouldn't wear girl jeans. My shirt was button-up, long-sleeve and white.

Lily fussed and unbuttoned the top three buttons and put on my blazer. She was more excited than me. Emmett banged my back with his hand. I swear, he could leave a mark if I weren't so resilient. I thought I looked silly when I checked the mirror by our door. The jeans and blazer thing was something for older guys with half-shaven beards, but whatever. If I looked stupid, it was all Lily's fault.

Grandma Rita nodded at me as Lily pushed me out the door. The outside was cold. I walked quickly and found myself at Kid's front door.

I knocked, and Virginia answered. She squinted and slammed the door.

A minute later Kid yanked it open and apologized for his sister. He was dressed in jeans and a bright yellow shirt and a black zip-up jacket — bee? anyone?

"No, it's fine. I did something to upset her, obviously."

Kid didn't answer me.

"Like my outfit?" I asked. "Lily spent three hours deciding on it. She's excited about this."

"Nice."

"Well, I suppose we should go watch the movie and get something to eat. Get our story straight." Funny the story is getting "straight." Maybe whoever made that saying up was a closeted gay.

"Yeah."

We walked in the direction of town. He didn't say anything. I looked at him. His face was scrunched up. "Is something wrong?"

He looked at me suddenly. "I really hate rule number two."

Rule number two was something very important for him, but I didn't get it. "Why? I just don't want you saying we're not friends."

"See... when I said that, I don't think you understood me."

"Then I must still not understand, because I'm completely clueless right now."

He stepped in front of me and stopped. "You really are that clueless? You swear?"

It felt like he was calling me stupid, but I couldn't help but nod. "I seriously don't understand what you're trying to say. I swear."

"Okay," he said and sucked in sharp breath. "I'm gonna clear everything up, and you tell me if you understand afterwards." He looked at the ground and then added, "I have to break rule number two, so don't get mad. If the rule still stands afterwards, I'll understand, but I've got to let you know."

I rose my eyebrows.

His hand hovered near my face. It seemed like he might hit me, but he just pushed my chin up

Him touching me made everything feel tingly. And I cursed that I liked him. He was being serious, and I was being gay.

He bent over so his face was really close to mine, and I wanted to kiss him, but I refused to let that part of me win. I tried to understand what he was telling me.

Then, it was over. Just as quickly and confusing as that. His hands were by his sides, and his fists were clenched. He looked at me and said in the most hopelessly small voice, "Do you get it?"

I could have laughed. If he was gay, I would've thought that he liked me or something, because if I got so close to someone's face, it'd be like I wanted to kiss them. But Kid was straight, and so I couldn't even mention my gay interpretation. He for sure wouldn't want to be friends with me if I liked him in a gay way. God, who knew being gay was so complicated? I shook my head.

His shoulders drooped, and he turned around and started walking in front of me.

"Kid," I said, grabbing his arm. "Can't you just tell me bluntly?"

He stopped and forced a smile. If the darkness hadn't messed with my eyes, I would've sworn he looked like he was about to cry. "I can't," his voice came out thin. "I just can't. I wish you'd understand and accept me."

"Accept you?"

"Yeah, accept what I'm trying to say, but I think that if you don't understand, then that means you don't accept it." He started walking again, and I strained to get my little legs to keep stride with him.

Accept it? My god, was this still about my sister? I mean, if he really liked her that much, then how could I get mad at him for that? I'd get over it if he decided to date my sister. I'd have to for us to stay friends. Gayness has no place in friendship. Yet, the thought of him with my sister was just so heart-breaking. But that'd be selfish of me to be jealous. I mean, I literally just became gay — or whatever the terminology is. I can't expect the first guy I like to reciprocate. I looked at the ground. "Kid, I know you're just trying to be considerate, because she's my sister and all, but I really have no problem with it. Every older brother feels protective of his sister, but I'm assured of your good guy-ness, so I'll be fine with it."

He didn't respond. Neither of us spoke until we arrived at the theater, where I paid and we went in. The movie was okay. I watched, but I kept thinking about us kissing. Man, I'm like a little love-drunk girl. And that made me feel stupid.

In the restaurant, we got a mixture of looks from both the staff and the fellow patrons. Some were giddy smiles followed by elbow jabs and incognito pointing. Others were completely indifferent, like us being there was no different from normal life. Others still were threatened. All were, of course, covert.

Kid was suddenly shy.

"You're so the girl," I joked, because I felt like the girl. God, man, my gayness would make this awkward. I was sincerely glad that he didn't know, because that would completely ruin our friendship.

He just looked at me and didn't respond.

"You're so gay," I said it, because straight guys did this kind of thing.

"Yeah."

Well, he wasn't making teasing him very fun. "Is something wrong?" I asked.

He looked away from me and shook his head.

That definitely made it seem like that something was wrong. "Don't lie," I said.

He forced a smile. "Really, nothing is wrong."

I let it go, for the moment. We ate our food, and he walked me back to my house, though I should have walked him back since I was the one taking him on a date — a fake date, but still. He held hands when we were in view of the windows.

I laughed. "It was fun, Kid. You are a very good fake boyfriend if I do say so myself." The bravado is key to maintaining my straightness.

He smiled half-heartedly, probably pining after my sister.

I winked at him. "Dude, I'll put in a good word in for you with my sister."

He shook his head. "No, don't do that."

"Oh, so, you're one of those suffer-in-silence types, huh?" I let his hand go and banged on his back as hard as I could. "You're totally smitten, man. It's embarrassing that you're so obvious. Totally not manly. Grow some balls and ask her out." Of course, that would be weird when she thought he was dating me, but I'd be willing to lose the guise of our relationship if Kid didn't want to anymore.

He shook his head but pulled me into a bear hug. It made me feel warm. Funny, how a totally manly guy like him could do something so gay and still not be gay, like my dad. If I did that, it'd be like a blaring Las Vegas sign. I watched him walk away.

An enthusiastic squeal was ready and raring to go when I opened — and securely closed — the door to my house. A fake date was too overwhelming for my heart. But my light heart was met with something I didn't want or expect.

Grandma Wendy's arms were crossed over her chest unlike their usually open and beckoning out-stretching. Her eyes bore down on me, but she wasn't speaking to me. " – s going to Hell. You cannot seri-ously encourage this blasphemy. God will punish every single last one of you for standing by and let-ting this happen."

"Mom, you are not welcome here if you continue speaking like that." It was my dad.

"This is not right. God will strike him down. I'm trying to save his soul... and yours."

This earned a quick retort from Emmett. "No, you think you are, but really you're trying to save your own soul."

Grandma Wendy ignored this and continued with her speech.

She must have been monologuing for quite some time, because Emmett and Dad were the only ones still arguing with her. Lily and Mom were curled onto the couch together, eyes closed. Grandma Rita and Grandpa Vin were gone, on their way home probably. My uncles and their wives and children were presumably sleeping. At least, I would have hoped that Grandma Wendy had been monologuing for an inordinately long time, because if everyone cared that little to not stay and defend me, it would have made Grandma's repudiation of me that much worse.

Emmett turned to me, ignoring Grandma. "So, how was it?"

I almost didn't have the heart to exalt my joy but Kid hugging me completely outweighed my disownment. "I really like kissing," I didn't exactly lie. I just let on that we had kissed.

An approving grin spread across his face. "Did you even see the screen?"

It took a moment for me to get what he was saying, and I chose to capitalize on it. "I know what happened in the movie, but he did let me touch him all over." I added this for Grandma's benefit.

And if she hadn't been right there, I'm sure he would've burst out laughing. He wiped away a nonexistent tear. "My little boy's growing up. Already to the groping stage."

I tried to throw him my most deadly look, but I've never been particularly good at that. I turned to Grandma, who had spoken all throughout the little exchange between my cousin and me. I cleared my throat. "I kissed a boy, and damn, did I like it." Yep, I actually said that. I'm not one for assessing the situation or treading carefully. I'm all for instant gratification, and that felt phenomenal, regardless of future consequences. "Hi, Grandma." Yeah, I can't show even a sliver of weakness against her verbal siege, because she knew she couldn't wiggle her way under my dad's skin. But if she thought she could do that to me, she would lie in wait, and bide her time, and whisper and shout and sing her word of God to me until I was putty in her hands.

I knew my Grandma, even if her fury had never before been directed at me. I knew her. I remember the time two years ago at Uncle's house when she was angry at the delivery man. She kept him at our Uncle Thomas's door until well past sundown — no, not for the whole day, but for a good hour. He squirmed and writhed, but she just didn't stop. I don't know why he didn't just leave, but he didn't. He looked like he had gone through a blender afterwards. Insulted, prodded, belittled, scoured until he bled. She finally let him go, and he apologized profusely. It was weird.

I pushed past her and spread myself out on the couch. My bravado was wearing off, but I smiled up at her.

Her mouth involuntarily twitched. She said something that I ignored.

"Grandma? Do you want to meet him?" I asked. "You'll like him." I closed my eyes. "Grandma, he's beautiful."

"God will punish sinners."

"Grandma, something as beautiful as him can't be a sin." Bravado was back in full swing. I think I'm a sadist. I was enjoying making my grandma uncomfortable. I showed my teeth. "Hot as Hell, Grandma."

"David, control your son." I opened my eyes to see her hands shaking.

"Grandma, you want me to tell you how it felt when we kissed? His lips are like candy. Oh, Grandma, his chest is hard as rock."

Emmett's laughter boomed in my bones. I grinned at him. Dad looked so confused. For once, he wasn't on the in.

"Grandma, haven't you ever loved your best friend?" Saying that hit me somewhere in the gut. It was true.

"Never."

"Grandma, that's sad indeed. Grandma, it's a high. I'm a birdie. You should be a birdie." I wasn't entirely acting. Of course, the weird voice and giggles were entirely fabricated, entirely.

She smacked me. I've never been smacked, and her swift hand felt like a whip. I almost jumped out of my skin and smacked her back, but I stopped my hand. It stung. Though my cousins' hits hurt more physically, this was another class that was so much more painful. My eyes felt watery, and I blinked furiously. I lowered my voice. "Leave, right now." I held my hand up to my dad. "Dad, don't say a word." I stood up and looked at

Grandma. "I was being nice and funny."

She didn't move.

I grabbed her arm roughly and started to tow her to the door.

She hissed and withdrew her arm.

I sighed. "You can't catch gay." But in that moment, I sincerely wished that you could. My poor grandma.

~

My dad's side of the family and us were all there at the table swirling our Cheerios around. The sun peeked into the dining room. Emmett was the only one who looked cheerful.

Christmas Eve is supposed to be more... something better than this.

And I had strategically chosen a seat next to my Grandma, which made it even worse. Last night, I had gotten her to the door, and I should've kept my resolve. But I saw her eyes which didn't look as angry as scared. It's the one time I've ever had any sort of conscience. God, why am I such a good person?

I passed her the pitcher of orange juice, and she glared at me while taking it. Yeah, maybe I should've made her leave. She wasn't going to change and suddenly accept me when I barely accepted myself. Naw, I love myself, but I'm sure straight guys don't suddenly have a fake boyfriend after being friends for a month and feel comfortable with it off the bat.

The day after Christmas my family left. Nothing changed. Grandma didn't suddenly have an epiphany. Jack didn't even look in my direction — my feeling is that Jack is so deep in his closet that he doesn't know it himself, haha. Peter only spoke to me when he needed to. Shelby had only put whip cream in my hand while I was sleeping. It was her first harmless and relatively funny prank on me. It was actually cute. Ryan was cute, too. He tried not to blush when Lily, Emmett and I made gay jokes. Uncle Bennett made an effort, but I knew he only did it because Dad gave him that look.

Mom tried so hard. I caught her looking at me so many times, and when she realized she was being watched, she'd blink and smile at me. It wasn't religion for her, like it was for Grandma. Mom was just completely surprised and scared and thrown out of her element. It would take her a while to adjust.

Dad left three days after Christmas. He hugged me so many times that I think his arm prints are etched into my back. He whirled Lily around, and kissed my mom slowly. I turned away, feeling embarrassed, but Lily whistled. She's just as shameless as me, more shameless when it comes to stuff like this.

The house was quiet after he left. Everything seemed like it had been a dream. Kid was gone to his football camp. Dad was on his way back to China. Mom whipped out her Windex and cleaned the banister. Lily yacked to her friends on the phone upstairs in her room.

I didn't go upstairs to play *Call of Duty 4* like I usually would for the remaining of my break. I pulled on my jacket and told Mom I was going out.

God, it was cold. I ducked my head down and walked quickly. My walk, though hurried, was fairly aimless. I stopped by Ralph's to eat a Ding Dong — wow, that was actually unintentional.

I was about to go back when my phone buzzed with a text. It was from a blocked number. *Ur a pervert goddam homo.*

I deleted the message. A random stranger hating me wasn't as bad as my grandma doing the same thing. I turned and started walking home faster than before. The text bothered me, despite my rationalizations.

I got another just then: *rot in hell.*

Five more in total before I got home.

god hates you

ur a fag, cant even fight back

i bet you scream like a girl when hes sucking your cock

fags like u shud just die

respond basturd

I looked at my phone and just stuffed it back in my pocket.

My mom was working on the entryway floor when I opened the front door. I skidded around her and jumped up the staircase. I locked my door and put my phone on my bed.

It buzzed with several new messages that I knew were from the same person. I didn't even bother looking at the new messages. Instead, I hit the reply button and typed in: *Ah, gay sex is amazing. He's relentless, but I don't mind.*

The reply was almost instantaneous: *glen isn't on top you lying basturd.*

I looked at the message. Who was this guy? Of course, I'm full of bravado all the time, so I replied: *With me he is.*

I didn't get a response, so I knew I'd gotten to this guy. I typed in a new message: *Who are you?*

No response. The barrage had finished. I lay down on my bed and set the phone next to me.

~

The next day came at noon, and I was woken by my phone buzzing. I prepared myself for the nasty texts, but I was met with: *just wanted to say hi. so, hi.* It was from Kid, and I grinned like a fool.

I responded with my best nonchalant best friend reply, which turns out to be: *Hey, how's it going?*

It wasn't until I was downstairs, feeling happy-go-lucky and eating my breakfast-lunch combo — cereal and a sandwich — that I received a rather startling text: *im gonna fuckin kill you.* My stomach flipped upside down, and I frantically shut the phone off. I pushed my food away from me.

Two weeks. School started. The texts didn't stop, but of course I did my best to seem completely unabashed when I saw Kid again.

And since I was gay now, I recognized his supreme gorgeousness right away without my usual mental explanations to myself. I guess knowing it in my mind was better than denying it to myself. God, the way he held himself was beautiful. His shoulders curved slightly, but the rest of his back was straight and subtly muscular. And he has this sheepish grin. Which is adorable. It makes me smile that I can freely think about things like that now. It's amazing how many thoughts I've subconsciously avoided thinking.

"I've been craving one of these," Kid said when we got our burritos at the cafeteria.

I snorted. "Just like you've been craving my ass." Teasing Kid is too much fun, because he is too easy-going. I'm kind of a sadist, and I like to see people squirm.

He smiled and shrugged. "Well, your ass is hot."

What guy has the cojones to say that? I mean, a manly guy like him — it's not too far of a stretch that I'd say something outrageous.

"Eww." My sister popped up next to me. "You guys are just too gay."

Kid shrugged.

I acted appalled. "Gay? Me? Never." I used my free hand and patted Kid on the back. "Now, this guy here, I'm not sure about."

Lily rolled her eyes and was pulled away by one of her friends.

Kid and I sat at a table, and I looked seriously at him. I asked, "So, when are you going to ask her out?"

His eyebrows snapped together. "Who?"

"Lily."

"I'm not going to ask her out."

"But you like her," I said.

He shook his head.

I felt my phone buzz in my pocket, and my face felt tingly — Spidey senses, for sure. I ignored it. "Then, what do you want me to accept?"

He sighed and shook his head. "Nevermind, just forget it." He didn't say anything more.

I didn't push further, though I wanted to. I pulled my phone out and was assaulted by another text from the Homophobic Bastard. I hurriedly shut my phone and stowed it back in my pocket. Kid didn't notice.

After school, Kid and I walked home together. My phone buzzed three times, and I ignored it.

"Wanna come over?" Kid asked.

I shrugged and found myself teasing Allison by standing on my tip-toes and letting her jump to high-five me. The sad thing was that she could almost reach when I was stretching my body to its limits.

Virginia leaned against the wall with her arms crossed over her chest and watched me. Kid was in the kitchen, scaring up some snacks for us.

I stared at Virginia, and Allison smacked my hand hard. She laughed like the cutie she was. I felt her hug me. Virginia's face didn't soften or anything. She must have a heart of stone — the moment her sister and I had was adorable, c'mon. She glared at me. It was truly a death stare.

"Did I do something wrong?" I asked her. She liked me well enough when they first moved in, but now it seemed she loathed me.

She opened her mouth, but her eyes flitted to the kitchen. Kid emerged, and she closed her mouth.

I exerted all my strength and struggled to lift Allison up. She squealed. I said to her, "You like me, don't you?"

She grinned. "Yeah, I like you. You pay attention to me, not like Glen."

I laughed.

Kid snorted. "Yeah, well, who can do superman with you, hmm?" For the losers who don't know, 'superman' is apparently when Kid lies on the ground and lifts up Allison with his feet on her midsection and his hands in her armpits. It's quite a feat.

Allison stuck her tongue out at her brother. I set her down, and Kid and I went upstairs to his obsessively neat room.

Kid handed me a travel-size bag of chips.

I lay on his bed, not leaving him any room. "So..."

"Yeah?" he asked, sitting on his desk chair.

I rolled over and stared at him. "Why don't you have a girlfriend yet?"

He looked up from his food. "You know why."

I rolled my eyes. "No, I do not know. It seems like everything you try to tell me is in some cryptic language or something." Kid was beyond frustrating sometimes, ugh.

He groaned. "You can't be saying that you STILL don't get it."

"Why don't you just spell it out for me?" It was annoying. Why did he have to just keep me in suspense constantly? Did he know about my gayness? Was he trying to torture me because he knew my feelings?

His hand whacked down on the arm of his chair. "I can't. It's not just my embarrassment anymore. I'm giving you an easy out. I'm letting you pretend to be dumb, Warren. If I said it, we wouldn't be able to act like it didn't exist. I know that's why you are pretending. It's easier to just ignore it for both of us. But you're pushing me. That act is going too far. Stop being dumb."

I saw his hands shaking, and my stomach dropped. I'd never seen him so angry. It made me want to hold him, but I furiously blinked that urge away. I turned away from him and started to speak, "Kid, I've told you. I have no problem with you being with my sister." As I said it, I knew, in a very guttural sort of way, it was a lie. But what could I do? Any straight guy would have qualms about his sister dating his friend, but a straight guy would get over it.

His voice came out small and watery. "God, Warren. Just stop playing. Please. It's insulting." He didn't sound insulted; he sounded incredibly hurt.

I turned and faced him. It seemed like he was going to cry. I opened my bag of chips and started stuffing them in my mouth, not even caring that I was leaving crumbs on his bed. When I was done, I said, "How was football camp?"

~

The texts continued all the way into February. My phone would buzz in class and when I was at home. It would buzz when I was at Kid's house. No place was safe, and it seemed like a cowardly move to shut it off.

One night while eating a silent dinner with Mom and Lily, my phone buzzed. I didn't bother checking it, but my sister butted her nose into my business.

"Hey, loser, answer your phone. It's rude to ignore it."

"We're eating dinner," I countered. "It's rude to ignore you guys, idiot."

Mom smiled at both of us. "It's okay, Warren. You can answer it."

I stared at her. Now, I had to answer it. I sighed and pulled my phone from my pocket. It was the Bastard.

"Is Glen sexting you?" Lily asked, mischief in her eyes.

I forced my slyest grin. "Yeah, and it's more action than you'll ever get."

She rolled her eyes.

Mom asked a naïve question. "What's sexting?"

Lily and I both looked at her and didn't answer.

After dinner, Lily installed herself in my doorway and wouldn't let me pass.

"Move, you bitch," I said.

But she looked at me seriously. "What's going on?"

"Huh?"

"You looked terrified to look at your text."

I tried to look completely clueless, but she saw through me. Instead, I downplayed it. "It's nothing." I said it with as much resolution as I could muster.

She dropped her arm from the door jamb. "Fine, don't tell me." As she walked away, she elbowed me hard in the stomach.

I locked the door to my room and threw myself on my bed. I felt like crying and not because Lily's attack really hurt.

The next day, my phone buzzed non-stop. I actually had to turn it off when my third period teacher glared me down. When lunch came, I made my excuses to Kid and went to the bathroom. I locked myself in a stall and avoided a puddle of piss, the smell was putrid. When I was sure there was no one in there, I started to cry. I spat into the toilet and swore like a sailor. I wiped my eyes and silently scolded myself for being so weak. I left the stall. I had turned on the faucet when I heard a toilet flush.

Dean Sexton walked over to the faucet next to me. He scrubbed his hands slowly and methodically while looking at me through the mirror. As he walked behind me, I saw his hand linger above my shoulder in the mirror. Then, he was gone.

I swore and washed my hands and whipped out my phone. I read the texts from the Bastard and then turned it off.

Outside, Kid was laughing with Richard about something. Richard started when he saw me. "Hi," he said.

I looked up at the giant. I forced a smile. "Hi."

Kid put his forearm on my shoulder.

I grinned for real at Richard. "Did you grow more?"

Richard seemed to be in an astonishingly good mood, because he laughed. He's just too stoic a character to laugh, so yeah, he's got to be happy. "Maybe a few inches, huh?"

"More like a few feet, man," I said. "I feel like my hobbit status has just quadrupled."

"I called my sister," he said suddenly.

I was confused for a second, but then remembered. "Really? What'd she say?"

"I'm going to see her next weekend in LA."

"Awesome!" I held up my hand for a high-five, but instead of Richard's hand stinging mine, Kid's long fingers intertwined with mine. It felt like a jolt of electricity. He pulled my hand down.

I looked at him, and he shrugged.

Richard seemed suddenly uncomfortable and hurried off to somewhere.

Kid let go of my hand and quietly said, "Denise was watching us."

"Oh," I said. I looked down at the ground. "You know, we could stop pretending now."

"Why?" he asked. "It's funny." He seemed startled and tense. I don't think he thought it was that funny anymore. We'd basically shocked everyone we could. I liked it when he touched my hand when we thought someone was watching, but I knew he didn't reciprocate that excitement. He was just doing it as a favor to me. I mean, he shouldn't be the gay guy for all of high school. It'd be unfair to him.

"No, it's fine. I know it's not really funny," I said. "We should just tell everyone." I think I had an ulterior motive in saying this. I hoped that whoever was texting me would stop once they realized it wasn't real.

He grabbed my hand and squeezed my fingers. "I still think it's funny."

I stared at him. He was just trying to be nice. He probably knew that I liked him and was giving me a little of what I wanted. Kid is just that nice.

His eyes lit up; he grinned at me. "We just have to up the ante. We're not being shocking enough anymore."

I shook my head. "Man, it's fine – "

"We should make out in front of everyone. It'd be outrageous."

I shook my head. "Dude, I can't let you lose all semblance of masculinity just for my joke."

He let go of my hand. "Yeah. Dumb as always but not dumb enough. I almost forgot."

They say a woman's scorn is something to watch out for, but Kid's is so much more scary. He refused to talk to me for the rest of the day.

When I got home that afternoon, I turned my phone on and received five more texts from the

Bastard. A new one buzzed as I plopped down next to Lily on the couch. I ignored it, and she didn't say anything.

~

I slept like a log that night. My phone was off.

~

The next morning, my mom shook me awake. She informed me that Kid was waiting for me. I pulled my clothes on and brushed my teeth.

I rubbed my eyes and focused in on him. I blinked. It didn't look like Kid. He wasn't slouching or smiling or anything. He looked very serious. "Rule number one is broken."

I almost laughed.

"Today, I'm going to break both rules."

I squinted at him.

"Just today, and I'll be finished with my rule breaking. You will grant me that much, right?"

"O... kay."

He seemed relieved. He grabbed my hand and pulled me outside. His parent's station wagon was in the driveway. "My parents let me borrow it. Get in."

I climbed into the front passenger seat, and he started driving.

When I came back that evening, I felt like I had had fun, but I didn't understand why Kid did it. We basically just drove for hours and stopped at random places and talked about random junk. It was a pretty uneventful day hanging out, but Kid thanked me.

I do not understand him at all. I had lots of fun, and it made me like him even more — in a totally gay way, for your information. But it seemed to be really important to him.

When I collapsed back onto my bed, I turned on my phone which I had left on the charger in my room all day. Fourteen messages from the same person. It spoiled my mood.

I fell asleep, only to be woken up by my sister's fat ass on top of my back. She bounced a little to make sure she handicapped me. "So, are you lusting over how romantic he is?"

I didn't open my eyes. "Romantic?"

She snorted. "Uh, yeah, a surprise day trip is up there in romance."

I disregarded her and rolled over onto my back. She scrambled back up to sit on me. I struggled to breathe. And I cried. I don't know why I cried.

Lily started freaking out. "Did he dump you?"

I looked at her and nodded. Suddenly, I grabbed her and hugged her as close to me as I could. Tears were still coming, and I felt hopeless. Lily didn't resist me. She hugged me back and didn't say anything more.

Sleep and then screaming. YOU GODDAMN BASTARD! HOW DARE YOU? HE BAWLED HIS EYES OUT! YOU BETTER BE GLAD HE'S SLEEPING RIGHT NOW, BECAUSE IF HE WAS STILL CRYING,

I'D BE AT YOUR HOUSE RIGHT NOW PUNCHING A HOLE IN YOUR UGLY FACE!... DON'T TELL ME YOU GUYS DIDN'T BREAK UP! HE WAS CRYING! HE SAID YOU DUMPED HIM... DON'T GIVE ME THE SILENT TREATMENT, YOU BASTARD. YOU'RE THE ONE WHO CAUSED THIS. TAKE RESPONSIBILITY... COME HERE RIGHT NOW AND MAKE IT RIGHT!

I closed my ears and tried my damnedest to figure out my tears. Could it be the messages? No, that upset me a lot, but this was just unexplainable. It was like falling through endless darkness with not one hope of safety or an end.

A tugging at my shoulder. I turned over. Kid's face. I cried some more. What's wrong? I don't know. I'm crying. Is there something I need? I don't know. To stop crying, perhaps.

"I'm sorry." And I wrapped my arms around him. I said, "Is this rule number two?"

"Yes."

I pulled him to lie next to me, and he complied with my wordless tugging.

~

I woke from sleep sweating and breathing hard.

~

I turned my phone on. Three new messages and Saturday. I blinked and sat up stretching my arms. It

140

hadn't happened. Kid hadn't taken me for a drive. I didn't cry like a baby.

I looked over at my window. It was closed. I stumbled over and pushed it up. I sat in the window seat.

He wasn't in his room, but, being the totally gay and smitten guy that I am, I decided to stay and wait for him. In retrospect, it wasn't the wisest use of my time, because he could have been gone for some football thing and wouldn't return all day. I should have just texted him or something, but my phone felt dirty.

It happened to be Virginia that I saw first in Glen's room. I waved vigorously at her, but she completely ignored me.

Allison, Kid's younger sister, went into his room. She had a mischievous look when she came over to the window. She opened it. "Hi, Warren!"

I smiled. "Hi, Allison."

"Wanna come over?"

"And do what?"

"Give me a makeover!"

I snorted. I'd do a worse job than Shelby did to Lily. "I can't reall – " I stopped myself. I now had an excuse to go over to his house, even though he was mad at me. "What kind of makeover?"

"I was thinking of being a tiger!"

I laughed. "Okay, I'll come over. Right now?"

"Yeah."

God, it was fun. I basically drew random junk on her face, and she squealed with excitement. Virginia gave me her death stares when she walked past us, but I just smiled back.

Allison treated me just like a seven-year-old girl. Is that something gay guys just exude? Girliness?

Their mother, Rebecca, was home, and she laughed when she saw Allison. Her laugh rang out crystal clear and soft.

"Pretty bang up job if I do say so myself," I beamed up at her.

"A fantastic job. You should do makeup professionally," she told me, smiling.

I was surprised that she wasn't weirded out by the fact that her son's fifteen-year-old (boy) friend was playing makeup with her seven-year-old daughter, but she wasn't.

"So, where's K – Glen?"

"He went running with a few boys on the football team an hour or so ago."

"Oh, do you know when he's going to come back?"

"Soon, probably."

"Can I wait for him?"

"Of course."

I lay on their family room carpet with my eyes trained on the front door. God, he took a long time.

He was laughing when he opened the door. He waved and shut the door. When he spotted me, he froze. "Hi?"

"Hi, Kid." I grinned. I didn't even know why I was waiting for him. I just wanted him to forgive me. One day of no talking was more than enough for me. "Rule number two can be null and void if you want it to be. I'll try not to be so dumb."

He stared at me for a long moment and shook his head. "No, it's fine. You don't need to do that. I can handle it. I know you can't handle not having that rule."

My phone buzzed in my pocket and I reached out and grabbed his ankle. God, that phone gave me goosebumps. I shook my head. "No, I want it gone."

Kid laughed in a sad sort of way. "I know you don't. Stop trying to be nice."

God, he was beautiful from every angle. I wanted to touch him, inappropriately of course. I desperately tried to erase those thoughts. "Wanna hang out?" I asked.

"Uh, sure."

I pushed myself off the floor.

He played some random video game while I watched. He didn't say much and neither did I.

I drifted off into sleep, but my phone eventually buzzed and woke me. The sudden chill, though, was countered with warmth. I felt Kid's arms around me. Man, such a nice dream. I touched his hand.

"Sorry," he said and pulled away from me.

I lay there until the dream ended and I woke up. Kid wasn't in his room anymore. I slid down and started clumsily playing the game.

Kid came and sat next to me. He put a sandwich on a plate next to my feet and then chomped on his own sandwich. "Sorry," he said quietly.

"For what?" I asked. Did he know the dream I had? Did I talk in my sleep or something?

"Never mind," he said. He seemed angry again.

I put my hand on his arm, and he shook it off.

My phone buzzed, and I got up and went to the bathroom. Another message from the Bastard. I gritted my teeth and replied, *Leave me alone*.

The reply? *no*.

I swore as quietly as I could and shoved the phone back in my pocket. I ripped the door open and met Virginia's accusing eyes. I pushed past her and sat right next to Kid in his room.

I put my head on his shoulder and laughed. "Best gay lover ever."

He stiffened and shook me off. "Stop with the gay stuff. If you're gonna play dumb, then don't tease me like this."

So, he knew... that I liked him? I scooted away from him and apologized. I felt like crying. I didn't, of course. That would have been gay.

When I left that evening, I didn't feel happy at all. I felt way worse, and on top of it, the texts were getting more frequent.

Lily hogged the TV, and I ended up watching more *Drop Dead Diva*.

"Lily," I said in a small voice. "What if I told you that me and Kid were never really together? And that Kid is straight, and he really likes you?"

She squinted at me.

"And what if it turns out that I really am gay and I love my fake boyfriend?"

She didn't say anything.

"And he knows it, that I love him. And, god, Lily, I feel miserable."

She snorted. "Nice try, but I see he loves you. What's the real reason you were scared of answering your phone?"

I glared at her and sighed. "You're an idiot."

~

Monday morning, I walked to school by myself. My phone hadn't buzzed with a message from the Bastard since Sunday morning. So, when my phone rang with a call, I answered it.

"Hello, Warren," said a smooth voice on the other end.

"Hello? Who is this?"

"God hates you, fag. He's gonna strike you down any day now, and if he doesn't, I will. Yo – "

I hung up. It felt like someone had just punched me in the gut, but I kept walking to school.

When fourth period ended, I slowly put my stuff away. Mr. Werely looked at me. "Is everything alright?" he asked.

I threw him an obligatory half-smile and nodded my head. "Yeah." I'm the ultimate hero. I keep it all bottled up inside. The chicks would totally dig me, especially because of my gay status. Girls love the gay guys, because we're just so approachable and non-threatening. Actually, it'd be funny if someone like Richard was gay, because he'd scare everyone off. I managed to muster up a laugh of sorts and decided to mess with Mr. Werely. I guess I'm not the ultimate hero. I'm a sadist. I smiled at the teacher and grabbed a chunk of my hair. "You've heard, I'm sure?"

"Hmm?" Mr. Werely snapped his attention away from his computer.

"That I'm gay?"

Mr. Werely just stared at me.

"Anyway, there's this guy that I really like. He has brown hair, brown eyes, medium height." I stepped over to my teacher. This was completely inappropriate, and that's why I did it. Then, I did my best to blush. I don't know if it worked, but I sure felt embarrassed. "He actually looks kinda like you." I threw in a girlish giggle to seal the deal. "Anyway, I was wondering if you had any tips on how to tell him that I like him. I don't know if he's gay."

Mr. Werely backed up a respectable distance. He seemed really uncomfortable, but his face did not reveal it at all. "Who is he exactly?" his voice squeaked.

Then, I stopped dead in my tracks. I very well couldn't think of anyone off the top of my head. I chuckled. "Just joking, Mr. Werely."

"Excuse me?"

"Just trying to freak you out, sir." I snorted. Then, my chest caught. "But, but…" I love Kid? No, I didn't want to say that. It wouldn't make sense. I was already "dating" him. I'm getting harassed? No, there would be calls made, especially with a man like Mr. Werely involved.

He looked like he was trying to process what I had just said. I'm sure no student of his had ever had the nerve to insinuate a crush on him, even if I took it back. Nonetheless, he looked me dead in the eyes with such compassion that it panged my heart.

I looked away and was surprised to find my eyes feeling watery. "Shit."

A box of Kleenex hovered beneath my noise. "This is a safe place."

Which was ironic, because the next second Kid's voice rang clear through the room. "War – ... ren?"

God, he looked amazing, slightly silhouetted in the doorway.

I shoved the box of tissues away from me. Within a moment, I had my backpack slung over my shoulder while I walked out onto the quad. I did my best to wipe my eyes incognito.

But Kid had seen. "What's wrong, man?"

I looked up at him and smiled as best I could. "Nothing." I laughed in a hollow sort of way. "Just that time of the month."

It took him a millisecond to comprehend and then he stopped. "Really, no jokes."

I shook my head and kept walking.

His hand on my shoulder felt like I was suddenly trying to walk through set concrete. "Warren, I'm your best friend. Tell me."

I shook my head. "Naw, it's okay. You said no gay crap. Well, I'm going to respect your rule," I kind of snarled it, though I had no real right to be mad at him.

He dealt with my rules. Just that call from the Bastard rattled and upset me to my core, on top of my totally obliterated feelings for my best friend.

"Warren?" Kid didn't let go of me.

I ripped myself free from him. "Just fuck off, Kid. Fuck off. You've made yourself very clear. Crystal clear. Your rule stands. I won't push it. So just... fuck off." I think I had a combination of spit, snot, and salty tears on my face. I ran away from him. And he must not have followed, because I was sure he was a lot faster than me.

I ran out of the gates of the school. God, god, god. I slowed, but I didn't stop. My sneakers slapped the ground in a very rhythmic way. The cuts in the concrete of the sidewalk moved past me.

I didn't really pay attention to where I was going, but I made sure not to go to the criminal parts of town. I'm not stupid. Blonde and brunette bimbos in movies always run and cry and wind up in the bad part of town, but this wasn't a movie. It was real life. Real people aren't so stupid. Movies need those bimbos to create damsels-in-distress that need rescuing by the superhero. Then, the bimbo and hero hold each other, and everyone lives happily ever after. Except I'm not so lucky to be so dumb. No happy ending for me. Instead, I'll have to see a therapist every week for the next two years, because Mr. Werely thinks I have self-esteem issues. And Kid won't be my friend anymore, because he really can't deal with my feelings. My mom will flit around like the terrified bird she is, and Dad will say that he loves me unconditionally. Lily will snicker and punch me in the gut. Grandma will be self-righteous.

And it'll drive me crazy. The more I talk to the therapist the more I'll get excited about the idea of a hot bullet sliding out of a cool barrel. And then when I'm twenty — because I've agonized over the decision for so long — I'll pull the gun out of the sock drawer.

My phone rang. I froze. The back of my neck tingled, and I slowly reached into my pocket. When I answered the call, I started screaming. "You goddamn bastard. I hope you die. Better yet, I hope I get to meet you and rip out your tongue first. Then, I'll take a pair of snippers and buh-bye twenty-one of your favorite appendages. Then, you die, really slowly. I hope you're happy, bastard! Glen and I were never together or anything, you fag. He's straight as a pencil. I guess you picked the right one to harass, though. I'm as gay as roller-skating at the beach. I bet you're the faggiest fag lusting over him, though. Well, guess what, I kissed him. More than you'll ever get to do. And guess what, God hates you. You're gonna burn in hell. Fuck you, bastard. You're less than shit." I threw my phone at the ground.

It didn't smash dramatically like in the movies. But the rage was still boiling in me so I stomped it with my foot until it really was just a collection of loosely-connected circuit boards.

The barista inside the Starbucks I was standing next to just stared at me. A man laden with a rather large order of various coffee drinks stopped in front of me, letting the door of the

Starbucks slam. "Are you okay? Should I call someone?"

The blood rushed to my face, and I shook my head. "Sorry."

I stalked off. My stomach tied in knots, but it felt like a huge weight had been lifted off my shoulders. He couldn't call me if I didn't have my phone.

I giggled, happy that I broke it.

~

It was dark when I walked back to my house. As I got closer, I saw Kid sitting on the lowest step. His knees were spread apart with his head and shoulders sagging between them.

I stopped in front of him. "Sorry for getting mad," I said and attempted to sidestep him, but his hand clasped around my shin.

He laughed. "I thought you were talking to me at first. And I felt like just dying. I think I understand now though."

"What are you talking about?"

"I called you."

"I, uh, lost my phone."

"No, you answered when I called."

"No – " I realized suddenly that I hadn't checked who the call earlier was from. I guess I really am a brunette bimbo.

He grinned up at me. "I'm happy now, though."

"That some random guy was sending me death

threats because he thought I was dating you?"

"No, that you're gay."

My stomach sunk. "Look, Kid, I told you I wouldn't do anything gay when I'm with you."

He pulled me down to sit. "I talked to Lily. So, you like me, right?"

I glared at him. "That's a pretty dumb question if you ask me."

"No, it's not. You still have been totally dense and stupid as to who I like."

I snorted. He was just treating me like a child. "I haven't. You're head-over-heels in love with Lily. I knew it from the very second I saw your binoculars."

"So, you do like me, right?"

"Yeah," I whispered back.

He laughed in an almost hysterical way. "Remember when you first gave me a tour of town? And we met Denise on the street? And you pretended to be my boyfriend?"

"I wasn't gay at that point, for your information."

He winked. "Oh, I believe you. So, anyways, when we were walking away and you were cracking up, you suddenly got worried that you'd ruined my reputation, right?"

I nodded.

"And what did I respond?"

I shrugged.

"I said, 'No one would believe I'm gay anyway.'"

"Okay... ?"

He stared at me. "You must be the most dense person on the planet."

"No – "

"I'm gay, Warren."

I shook my head. He was trying to empathize with me or something.

"Remember when you were messing around or whatever? I didn't know what you were really doing. I thought you were testing me, but it turned out we were competing on who could hold out longest. Anyway, you kissed me, right?" I nodded. "At the time, I thought you were having some weird kind of fun. I thought maybe you were trying to ask me if I was gay. And so I kissed you back."

I looked at him, and my stomach had this eerie feeling. "So, who do you like?" I didn't want to hear the answer. It was already an impossibility that he was gay, but it was even more astronomically impossible for him to like me. So, I listed the most likely candidates. Richard, Dean... my dad? Please, if anything, not my dad. It'd be even worse than him liking my sister.

"You've got to be playacting, Warren." Kid put his arm around my shoulders. "No one is this dense."

"Just tell me it isn't my dad."

He gave a little laugh. "Not your dad." He slung his other arm across my chest.

I turned and faced him. His face was so close that I could feel his breath. "Me?" I asked it and hoped he wouldn't laugh. If it was just wishful thinking, I just wished he wouldn't think it absurd that I even entertained the thought.

He laughed.

152

About the Author

Georgia Tell lives in Los Angeles in a house full of animals: cats, dogs, lizards, rats and fish. When she's not writing books, she loves to knit, crochet, and create many elaborate financial spreadsheets. She also writes poetry.

www.GeorgiaTell.com
Twitter: @GeorgiaTell